To Walter

All the best/

writing. Night Osmoad.
.com

The Killing Breeze

The Killing Breeze

by

Tony Lindsay

Penknife Press   Chicago, Illinois

This is a work of fiction. The characters, dialogue and events described herein are the products of the author's imagination, and do not portray actual persons or events.

The lower socio-economic Black male is a man of confusion. He faces a hostile environment and is not sure that it is not his own sins that have attracted the hostilities of society. All his life he has been taught (explicitly and implicitly) that he is an inferior approximation of humanity. As a man, he finds himself void of those things that bring respect and a feeling of worthiness. He looks around for something to blame for his situation, but because he is not sophisticated regarding the socio-economic milieu and because of negativistic parental and institutional teachings, he ultimately blames himself.

Huey P. Newton, 1967

Chapter One

It was three o'clock in the afternoon. The blinds that hung in front of his room's only window were open. The afternoon sun flooded the studio apartment. It was a bright room without the sun. With the sun it beamed. The cherry wood bureau, table, and chairs gleamed in the sun's light. The walls and kitchen appliances were eggshell white. The chrome sink claimed as much sun as the cherry wood and bright walls. The room held the sun.

In the center of the room was a queen-sized bed. The frame of the bed was anchored to a cherry wood headboard. The frame held a box spring, a coil mattress, and him. At that time, his name was Maurice Davidson.

He was laid atop the bed, which was made in military fashion. A fitted sheet, a cover sheet, and brown cotton spread covered the coil mattress. He was grinning at the ceiling.

His two hundred pound, five foot ten inch frame covered a large portion of the bed. A white undershirt covered his muscular torso. His bottom half was covered by a pair of white sweatpants. His feet were in a pair of white high-top leather gym shoes. He wore no underwear or socks.

He had a grin across his face due to a solved dilemma. The problem was his hair. He wanted it to make a statement. He wanted it to say, "Fuck you." He tried braids and twists. None said it quite loud enough. When he woke that morning, the answer was clear. He cut it all off. He was so pleased with the image in the mirror that all he could do was grin. The baldhead was what he needed to complete his plan.

The date was August fourth 1991. He put it all together that day. Reform school, prison, and the state mental hospital were all training grounds for that day. He knows that now.

Reform school taught him how to say "no" when he was screaming, "yes" on the inside. Prison taught him how to say, "yes" when he wanted to scream "no" and "help." The state mental hospital taught him how to grin "yes" when he wanted to cry "no!" That day, he wouldn't say "yes" or "no." That day he would say, "Fuck you." That day, for the first time in his life, he followed his plan. Not the teacher's, the social worker's, or the gang's, his. The plan began in his mind five weeks earlier. It was his first session with the pretty parole officer.

For the first time in his life, he realized the problems of his life weren't his fault. Until that session, he always thought his misery was due to making wrong choices. He blamed himself for his poor reading skills. He blamed himself for joining a gang. He blamed himself for stealing. He blamed myself for being crazy. Others did; why shouldn't he?

He accepted the consequences of his actions with no complaints. He accepted the labels people applied to him: dumb, thief, drug addict, habitual criminal, and crazy. He was what people told him he was. He was sitting across the desk from his parole officer when a new label was applied.

"Institutionalized, that's what you've become, Mr. Davidson."

He didn't know what the word meant, but he knew it must have been negative because everything people told him he was- was negative. He asked the pretty, young, Afro-American female parole officer, "Who institutionalized me?"

She told him, "The system."

He asked, "Whose system?"

"Society's."

"Whose society?"

"This society here, white America's society, the white man's society."

The light went on in his mind that day and stayed on: the white man, the white man's society, and the white man's rules. He was a Black man. It wasn't his fault. He was in the wrong society. He was the wrong color for this society. If it were a Black society, the white man would be given a poor education. The white man would be dumb, crazy, a habitual criminal, and institutionalized.

White society had cheated him. White society owed him. It wasn't his fault. How was he supposed to play by their rules? They were white rules. He was Black. No one explained the rules until he broke them. It wasn't fair. They cheated him, and they owed him. They owed him for all the good things they kept away from him: a good education and a good job. They owed him for the life he didn't have. He was Black in a white society. It wasn't his fault, but that day, he would make it right.

He rose from the neatly made bed still grinning. He walked over to the cherry wood bureau and opened the top drawer. The drawer held one butcher's knife, a steak knife, and a roll of invisible tape. He pulled up his white undershirt and placed both knives behind the elastic waistband of his white sweatpants. He pulled his undershirt down concealing the knife handles. He held the tape in his hand. Still grinning, he turned and left the bright apartment.

Once on the street, he walked erect and deliberate. The grin was plastered on his face. It would be the first one: the first one that made eye contact, the first one that said something to him, the first one he heard, or the first one he smelled. It would be the first one.

Mexican, close.

~~~~~~

Arab, close.

Black, fuck.

White, blond haired, little boy with blue eyes, bingo.

The work was harder than he expected. The kill was easy enough, but the work; the work was much harder. Concentration pushed the grin from his face. It was messy delicate work, most definitely not to be done in an alley, but an alley was all he had. The trick was to find pieces big enough to wrap. He cursed himself for not bringing a pair of scissors, but how was he to know? He'd never done it before. White men knew how to do it, but they knew most things; it was their society.

The work took longer than he expected, but once finished, the grin returned to his face. Every part of his exposed skin was right now. Everywhere he looked, it was right. His arms were right, his fingers were right, his cheeks and his forehead were right. He was right.

No more misery, everything would be right because he was right. He walked from the alley with confidence and pride. Life was going to be better. No one would have dared call him dumb or crazy. With just one look, everyone saw that he was right.

He could have said, "Fuck you" without looking away. He could have said, "Fuck you" the way white men said it. He could have said, "Fuck you, nigger" and stared a Black man straight in the eye. After all, he was right. He was part of society. No more Black man in the wrong society. He was in the right society. No more unexplained rules. He walked from that alley reborn. He was right and white as any white man. Sure, he needed tape to hold the right skin on, but he would fix that; since he was white, he knew he should have used crazy glue.

That day happened twenty-three years ago. A lot has changed since then including his name. He is now Dr. Noble Breeze, a criminal psychologist with a removed past. That day has been erased from his life along with his conviction and sentencing to a mental institution. He owes his new life to the American Purist Society and Dr. Clarence Talbert, the psychologist who became his father.

Chapter Two

Doctor Breeze sits at his desk listening to a young student reporter, Denise Thomson. The student reporter is seeking a profile for a cop killer. She believes that a single killer has claimed the lives of three white police officers.

"My research shows that each local Falcon City cop shooting occurred after a Black person was reported shot or beaten by police. After each nationally televised incident, a Falcon City officer was killed."

She has spread news clippings across his desk in chronological order.

"The correlation is painfully obvious. I am certain the police have made it as well. I am hoping your profile will give me an edge for my story."

While looking at the news clippings and the notes on her open laptop, it becomes obvious to Breeze that the young student reporter has to be redirected. She is treading in dangerous waters. He understands why Melody directed her to him. Breeze looks up from the clippings and watches Denise Thomson unbuttoning her navy tweed jacket while adjusting in her seat.

"I was originally referred to Dr. Talbert, but his secretary redirected me to you. I hope that is ok? Do you think what I am saying is practical or even possible? Is this enough information to construct a profile?"

Breeze is curious about how she has profiled the killer thus far.

"Tell me, Denise, what type of person do you envision the killer to be? From what I have read, each officer was shot point blank in the head or chest. That says a lot to me. What about to you?"

Again, she adjusts in her seat and fiddles with the position of her laptop.

"Honestly, Doctor, and I hope you don't take offense, but I see an angry Black man doing this."

Breeze feels his eyebrows rise out of reflex. He restrains a smile.

"A Black man, really, why?"

"Because each Falcon City police shooting occurred after a Black person was beaten or shot by a white police officer."

Her stare is constant while she states her belief. Breeze appreciates her confidence.

"An Afro-American man, huh?"

He again looks down to her news clippings on his desk.

"Yes sir. That is what I believe."

"Interesting, and why would you think I would find offense?"

His eyes go to her laptop screen.

"Because you're Black."

He looks to her small face and sees her clear blue eyes looking at him intently.

"I am Afro-American, but I am not vested in each Afo-American's action. Would you be upset if the speculated killer turns out to be white?"

She smiles and says, "I see your point, Dr. Breeze."

"Good. In regard to the profile you are seeking and your perspective suspect being Afro-American – serial killers seldom kill for societal reasons. They don't kill to adjust wrongs larger than themselves. If they did, I think this country would have had many Afro-American, Japanese, and First Nation serial killers. This does not negate your theory concerning the same person is killing the officers, but I would hesitate to correlate the Falcon City police killings with national police misconduct."

"Why?"

She sits prone in her chair.

Because I don't want to kill you is Breeze's thought.

"Well, if the same killer is shooting police, he is doing it due to a personal violation. Somehow, he sees himself as being hurt by the police, and he is responding to that hurt. And again, if it is the same killer, he feels justified in that response. The killer feels entitled to his actions.

"Few Afro-Americans demonstrate feelings of entitlement in this country, and those that do have earned privilege from monetary gain, and they seldom act against the establishment. Once they are in the graces of privilege, they become almost silent.

"For the killer you are proposing to be Afro-American, his sense of entitlement would have to be close to permanent. The few Afro-Americans at that level seldom risk calling attention to themselves, and they are seldom disturbed about what happens to the masses of Black people."

She scoots to the edge of her chair and her eyes are tightening to near closed. Breeze sees wrinkles appearing across her forehead, and her lips are pressing almost into one.

"But what about a poor frustrated Black man who sees the injustice of the police misconduct and becomes fed up?"

Dr. Breeze smiles.

"You are making an assumption through empathetic eyes, as if you were a poor Afro-American male, but you can't fathom that position because you were born with white privilege, with white entitlement. From your white perspective, a poor Afro-American man would rise up and kill a police officer to balance the accounts.

"But from a Afro-American person's perspective, a frustrated individual would forgive and accept the injustice out of submission. This society has physically, mentally, and spiritually beaten Afro-American people into submissive conformity that causes them to think that the frustration is from within; something within them is wrong. They must be inept in some fashion, their poor societal status is due to something they did wrong, and thus they don't feel entitled enough to act out against what you as a white person sees as an obvious injustice. If a poor black possessed your sense of entitlement, then yes, your theory of an Afro-American killing in response to the police misconduct would be possible, but the current state of the Afro-American psyche in this city and country does not support your theory. My apologies.

"Based on the nature of the killings, the close range of the shootings, it is clear that the assailant felt confident enough to get face to face with the police officers. He felt equal to the officers if not superior. If there is a single killer of the police officers in Falcon City, he is a white male between the ages of twenty-five and thirty-five, and he feels greatly wronged by the police.

"I would start with children whose parents were slain by police, or children abused by the police or juvenile authorities. The quick succession of the killings indicates a lengthy suffering on the part of the assailant, decades would be my estimation."

Her face remains tight as she abruptly stands from his black nylon mesh backed chair. Dr. Breeze had to buy that chair himself; the University only furnished the hard wooden ones with no wheels and no seat cushion.

Denise Thomson is gathering her news clippings and closing her laptop.

"You paint a very bleak picture of Black and white people, Dr. Breeze."

"Really?"

He is smiling again.

With news clippings, papers, and laptop in her shoulder bag, Denise Thomson turns from him and progresses toward his office door.

He really likes her blue tweed jacket.

"I will invoice your paper."

"Yes, please do."

She snatches the office door open and leaves without another glance in Dr. Breeze's direction.

"Bye – bye," he says to the closing door. He doesn't hesitate in retrieving his keys from the desk drawer. He has a surprise for the child reporter.

Chapter Three

In the stairwell Denise says, "He must be what Jeremy calls an Uncle Tom and an Uncle Ruckus. How could he think Black people won't stand up for themselves?" A stairwell door on the flight beneath her opens, and she shuts up because she doesn't want people thinking she is Looney Tunes.

She overreacted and she knows it. Doctor Breeze's opinion has her taking the stairs down from his fifth floor office with shin splints. She wanted out of his presence as soon as possible, but each step down hurts, and the stairwell is extremely dusty. She overreacted because his opinion was so different from hers. She should have stayed and heard him out. That was the mature thing to do. Leaving annoyed was not a reporter's move. And there is the matter of his fee. As an intern at the paper, generating academic invoices is not part of her duties.

Jeremy specifically told her if there was a fee for the consult she was to walk away, but she wasn't sure about the fee until the end. Oh, well. She exits the stairwell into the dimly lit lobby of the building. She resigns herself with the thought that for a City University professor, Dr. Breeze is ignorant.

She exits the lobby through heavy oak and metal doors and walks into the afternoon sun. She stops on the stone stoop and takes in a deep cleansing breath trying to remove his aura from her person. After the sixth deep breath, she says to the universe, "That's better. Dr. Breeze is wrong; I know a Black man or men are shooting these police officers."

Her training watch reads 12:05. Mildred is covering for her another twenty-five minutes. She slings her shoulder bag crossways over her neck and briskly walks and runs down the Avenue towards Spring Grove. The #4 bus would drop her at the paper's door. If a bus is coming, she will be there in five minutes. Running will get her there in twenty. Her shins are opting for the bus.

She ran a lot the past summer, ten to twelve miles a day, and with autumn having been mild, she kept running, and with the winter being warm so far, running in the early morning remains an option. The school has a couple of indoor tracks, but she likes exercising outdoors, and she likes her outdoors in the city, not in the woods. Jeremy likes camping, and he has been trying to get her in the woods since the spring. "Nope, it's not going to happen," she says as if speaking to Jeremy

Denise decides to run full out to the bus stop to see how bad the shin splints really are. After a block, she feels that running isn't as bad as taking the steps down from Dr. Breeze's office. The traffic light caught her at Spring Grove, and she stops and runs in place.

She sees the southbound # 4 bus; it is two blocks down.

Jeremy agrees with her that the killer is Afro-American, and he agrees that the killings are in response to white officers killing Black males. It was Jeremy's idea to talk to psychological profile.

A dark blue detective's car has pulled alongside of her at the light, and the window is being powered down.

"Ms. Thomson, Denise Thomson?"

She stops running in place and faces the car.

"Yes?"

"Can we get a moment of your time?"

Police make Jeremy nervous. And for good reason, due to the police shootings, the city police, the county sheriff, and state police are patrolling the streets like ants on dropped candy, and reports of Afro-American citizens being harassed are at an all-time high. When she is with Jeremy, she is nervous about being in police presence as well. But alone, the police don't bother her at all. She isn't nervous in the slightest.

"Sure."

The detective backs up from the corner and parks behind her. She walks back to their blue unmarked sedan. A redheaded driver rolls his window all the way down, and she walks directly to it.

"I am Detective Fredrick, and this is Detective Owens," he says pointing his thumb to the officer next to him. "The lady at your office told us we could find you here. She did a real good job of describing you."

He is talking about Mildred. Denise smiles. Mildred is a very detailed person.

"Cool. How can I help you, officer?"

"You called the Division two days ago, and you left some very interesting questions. We'd like to discuss them with you, and maybe answer a couple."

Detective Fredrick has green eyes and serious plaque buildup between his two bottom center teeth. He needs to make an appointment with a dental hygienist. Denise wasn't expecting a call back from the police. She left the message out of protocol. The automated voice said leave one, so she left one, thinking that would be the end of it. The questions she left were her rambling, her constructing her thoughts and ideas. She really didn't think another human would listen to them, never mind seek her out to discuss them.

"Cool, we can talk while you guys drop me back at the office? Mildred is waiting for me."

"She told us," Detective Fredrick says, and he pops the lock on the rear door.

Denise gets in the back of the sedan and closes the door.

Detective Fredrick asks, "How did you end up interning at 'The Blackman's Journal'?"

The detectives' car smells like Jeremy's running shoes; he refuses to put baby powder or baking soda in them. Denise doesn't see any running shoes or sweat socks on the floor of the car, so she guesses that one of the detectives has hygiene issues. The one in the passenger seat, Detective Owens, is the gruffer of the two. A perspiration ring is edging the collar of his blue shirt. What a pair, one needs his teeth cleaned the other is smelly.

"My boyfriend works there. His dad is the owner-publisher, and I was looking for an internship, so he arranged an interview with his dad. Actually, I am their first intern."

"Are you the only white person working there?" Detective Fredrick asks while pulling the car from the curb.

"Pardon?"

"I mean . . . I have never seen any white people go in there. And it is called 'The Blackman's Journal.' So I am wondering, are you the only white person working there?"

Thinking, she pauses and tells him, "I could be Black."

Detective Owens sits up straighter in his seat.

"That is true. She could be. I know of a lot of Black people who look white."

Denise asks, "And do you know some whites that look Black?"

"Huh?" comes from Detective Fredrick.

His "huh" makes her laugh.

"Isn't it funny how we never think about the white people that look Black?"

"You mean those white people trying to be black?" Detective Owens asks.

"No. I'm talking about white people with large lips, curly hair, large butts, dark skin, Greeks, Italians, Jews, and Spanish people. All those whites that look Black or I should say African. My girlfriend, Nadine, refuses to wear pants because she gets tired of hearing that she has a Black girl's butt. She's German and wide hips with round buttocks are a female trait in her family, but here in America, she has a Black girl's butt. Am I making sense?"

"Sorta, but about the questions you left on the phone?" Detective Fredrick asks.

Denise figures her statements must be making him uncomfortable, since he is getting back on topic.

"Tired of talking about white people that look Black?"

He stops at the traffic light, "Sorta."

Outside the detectives' car, Denise sees a Falcon City police SUV and a squad car has pulled over and stopped two young men in and old '78 Cutlass, just like the one her father keeps under tarps in his garage. One of the officers has his gun out and is shouting orders at the boys. She pushes the button to roll her window down, but it remains up. She can't hear what the officer is yelling, but the boys are exiting the car with their arms up. They drive past the scene.

"Hey Fredrick," Detective Owens says turning his gaze away from uniformed police and the youth, "did you know I was Black? Yeah, the story is it that my great, great grandmother was the master's slave child, but she married his brother's son, and they had white babies. You couldn't tell they were Black until you looked at the male boy's privates. Yep, we still have the affliction today, big black shlongs."

"Oh, my God, Owens, please shut up. Just shut up – stop talking," Detective Fredrick orders.

"Why? It's true. I'm just saying. When I was in the army, the doctor almost marked me as colored guy after he saw it."

"Please, Mahoney, and I am sure Ms. Thomson is not interested in your lies."

Denise turns her attention back to the detectives, and to make them both uncomfortable, and because she doesn't like people speaking for her, she says,

"Yes, I am. Let me see it," and leans forward toward the front seat.

"Ok, ok, that's enough, both of you stop it." Detective Fredrick exhales. "Ms. Thomson, based on the questions you left on my voicemail, it's obvious you think the policeman that have been murdered here in Falcon City are related to the police-involved shootings across the nation?"

Detective Fredrick just irritated her. She leans back from the detectives and sits as erect as possible; her lower back and neck are tightening.

"Why do you call the police being killed here in Falcon City murders, while referring to the deaths the officers caused across the country as police involved shootings? The police murdered: Eric Garner, Tyree Woodson, Michael Brown, Ezell Ford, and Kajieme Powell; they were murdered too."

"No, those were police-involved shootings, officers trying to do very difficult jobs made harder by the bleeding heart liberal press." Detective Owens argues while making eye contact with her in the rearview mirror.

Staring back at him in the mirror, she has a thought, it tells her not to comment, to look away, to hear him out before she speaks, but she hears herself saying, "Fuck that, they were murdered, shot down like animals by fucking militarized police. The police in this country have lost their fucking minds and the whole world knows it."

The 'F' word comes when she's angry, and at times she can stop it, but this obviously isn't one of those times.

"Do you kiss your mother with that mouth? Jesus," Detective Fredrick commented.

"Not her mother, but I bet you a twenty-spot to doughnut she has a spade boyfriend she kisses with it," Detective Owens' eyes are back on her in the rearview mirror.

"Spade? Is that an attempt at insulting my big dick black boyfriend?" She says starring straight into the mirror.

His eyes leave hers.

She chuckles and looks away from the mirror.

"We came to see you, Ms. Thomson, because it occurs to me that you may have information about the killer or killers of these officers," Detective Fredrick announces.

The car stops.

She doesn't look out the window to see where. She is staring at the back of the Detective Fredrick's red head.

"What?" She asks.

"You made some very . . . stark correlations. A day after Eric Garner was killed, Officer Davis was shot in the face. One day after Tyree Woodson was shot, Patrolman Smith was shot in the head, and following the Mike Brown shooting, Patrolman Sanders was shot five times in the chest. The same with the Kajieme Powell shooting, a day later Patrolman Jackson was shot in the temple. After Ezell Ford, Detective Henry was shot in the face. Whether correlation or coincidence, your observations warrant investigation. My question to you - is it merely observation and theory or has someone shared with you some information, or have you overheard something that has given your theory legs? Do you have anything to support your beliefs that these police murders are related to the nation's police-involved shootings? Any at all?"

Fredrick has turned around completely in his seat to face her. She blinks her eyes when she is shocked, and the blockhead detective has just shocked her, so her eyes are blinking non-stop.

"Are you asking me if someone has confessed to killing these police officers, or if somehow I have been privy to the conspirators organizing these crimes?"

The detective looks at her without answering.

"Are you serious?"

He exhales, "What I am asking is, what do you know, if anything? What reasons do you have for making such harsh correlations? What evidence supports what you believe? This is what I need from you."

The police deaths in the city do have the cops on edge; more people are being pulled over and arrested. Jeremy tries not to drive. Yesterday, the Falcon City Tribune recorded that filed claims of police harassment were at a record high, so she understands that cops are stressed, but this guy is a supreme blockhead.

"Detective, I have no evidence. All I have are questions. I wanted to know if you guys see the correlation, if you think it is a possibility? But honestly, after meeting with Dr. Breeze, I have my doubts about the theory or story."

And looking out the window, she sees they have gotten her to the office.

"Is there anything else, Detective?"

He reaches back and hands her his card.

"Please, stay in touch."

She takes the card and exits the detective's sedan. She slams the car door by accident, not out of anger, but from annoyance at both Dr. Breeze and the police officers. She flips his business card back through the passenger window and walks to the office's glass door and yanks it open.

Foster Knight, the publisher of the 'The Blackman's Journal' brags about having the only glass front business on the block. Inside, Denise steps around the front counter and walks back to Mildred's desk. She smells the jasmine potpourri Mildred has in the small crockpot in the corner. She drops down into the brown, aluminum, folding chair on the side of the beaten-up pine desk.

Mildred is looking out the front window smiling.

"You got the po-poes to give you ride, huh?"

The detective car drives off.

"Yeah that was least they could do, bastards."

Over the potpourri, she smells hamburgers.

"The only place they ever took me was to jail. Must be nice having them provide a service."

"It didn't feel like a service. It felt like an interrogation. My questions, the ones I left on the voicemail, made them think I know something about the killer or killers."

"Maybe you do." Mildred says, raising the white bag from the chair on the other side of her desk. "Hungry? Jeremy got burgers for everybody. His dad was pissed, though. He said the paper can't run on trade. The restaurant manager was to pay for last month's ad. Jeremy got half the payment, a promise to pay, and double cheeseburgers. I thought that was pretty good, but Mr. Knight didn't. He started yelling and Jeremy left to get drinks."

24

She pushes the picture of her twin ten-year-old boys aside and places the sack of burgers to the side of her computer screen.

Denise' boyfriend hates arguing, so he leaves when his father explodes which happens whenever the Journal's finances are discussed. The paper isn't broke, but it is not turning a profit either. Her internship is unpaid.

Looking at Mildred, Denise wishes her eyes were big and brown and round like Mildred's. Denise's mother gave her blue eyes. Mildred is twenty-five but looks seventeen, largely due to her youthful big doe eyes and dark-brown almost black cornrow braids. Mildred pulls a burger from the sack and puts it in front of Denise.

"Dr. Breeze didn't think much of our theory," Denise sighs.

Mildred knows of the theory because most of it was formed at the next desk over; the work desk that Jeremy and Denise share. Mildred helped form it with Jeremy and Denise, and she is just as confident in it as they are.

"Who?" Mildred is opening the yellow wrapper of her own burger.

"The City University professor I ended up speaking with."

"That's funny. There is a Dr. Breeze in the back, talking with Mr. Knight."

Denise turns to look back into the press area, and standing over the layout table eating a burger with Mr. Knight is Dr. Breeze. Both men have shaved baldheads and the sun's beams are shining through the skylight onto their crowns.

"What the fuck?" she asks, looking right at him.

Looking back to the pressroom, Mildred says, "He walked in a couple of minutes before you. Same guy?"

"Same fucking guy."

Chapter Four

Dr. Breeze sees the little white girl staring at him with her mouth hanging open. He doesn't fight the impulse and smiles at her. He and the publisher, Knight, are working on a committee to stop the public school closings in the Burnham neighborhood of Falcon City. They graduated from undergrad together. Knight was a journalism major who thought he could change the world by finding the truth and sharing it. Breeze thought he was foolish back then because he had never known the truth to change anything.

He believed powerful people knew the wrong that they did and what they were getting away with, and the weak already knew the truth because they were living it, but life has taught him different. The truth can change things. He has seen it empower the weak by merging them into a cohesive unit. He has seen the weak rally around a truth, and force it down the throats of the powerful changing the weak to the powerful.

"Your intern came to see me today," he tells Knight while looking at the little white girl.

"My what? Oh, the office-kid, yeah about what?"

"The cop killing story you guys are working on."

He looks away from her and down to his cheeseburger. Her questions could be a problem if she gets others investigating the correlation. His assigned tasks could become difficult. He needs to know the paper's stance. He looks up from the burger to Knight.

"What cop-killing story? We're not working on a cop-killing story, not to my knowledge. Maybe Jeremy has got her on it. He's the senior editor; most of the copy is left to him. I'm trying to turn over the whole paper over to him, but the boy has a problem counting money."

"Well, she approached our department chair, Dr. Talbert, about it and got referred to me for the consult."

"Really? Are consults free?"

"No, but for you, you know."

"Thanks, Breeze."

"So, you haven't heard her theory?"

"No, but my son is no slouch. If he ok'd it, she must be on to something."

Knight has worn cardigan sweaters and jeans since their college days. If Breeze didn't know better, the yellow sweater Knight is wearing now could easily be mistaken for one worn back then. He wore the elbows out of them then much like he's doing now.

"Denise, come back here for a minute." Knight yells to the little white girl.

"Sir?" she answers.

"Come."

She stands from her chair and walks towards the two men. Breeze takes another bite from the cheeseburger. He is really enjoying it.

"You went up to the University seeking a consult?" Knight asks Denise.

"Yes sir, with Jeremy's approval."

"Hmmph, my son thinks we are made of money. We're not," Knight tells her. "You both got lucky this time. Dr. Breeze is a friend of mine and the paper. Let me hear your theory."

The girl looks from Knight to Breeze and back to Knight. If she answers with the same determination and conviction she possessed earlier, she will establish herself as a problem for Breeze, one that will have to be dealt with.

"Well sir, it was an observation more than a theory. It became a theory through discussions with Jeremy and Mildred. It started after the Eric Garner and Tyree Woodson shootings. I mentioned to Jeremy that after each shooting a police officer was shot here in Falcon City. We both thought it was coincidence until Michael Brown was murdered. After that we brought Mildred into the conversation. All three of us hoped there wouldn't be another shooting. We didn't want the correlation to pan out. But sadly, Ezell Ford and Kajieme Powell were killed, and after each death, a day later, a white Falcon City police officer was shot dead.

"I went to up to the University looking for collaboration; to see if there was a profile for a person who kills in this manner."

Knight looks at her pensively while stroking the stubble on his chin.

"No. I don't see one person doing this; perhaps an organization like the Panthers or the Weathermen of the past; but today, in this passive and bought-off society, people are concerned only with their individual struggles. Me, me, me is the age we live in. What did Dr. Breeze tell you?"

She looks to Breeze.

"Pretty much the same as what you just said, sir; only with stronger racial connotations. He doesn't think Blacks feel privileged enough in this society to kill police."

She is still looking at Breeze, and he interprets her gaze as her thinking he is an idiot. Yes, she is a problem, he thinks.

"And what do you think?" Knight asks her.

Before she can answer, Jeremy runs through the front door yelling.

"Oh my God! They just released a video of the 12-year-old that was shot Saturday in Cleveland. The police shot him down in the park!"

Breeze's recognizes Jeremy. As a kid, he was curious and robust and always cheerful. His birth caused the death of Knight's wife. Breeze remembers it was difficult time for his friend. Jeremy looks like his deceased mother, same charcoal dark skin and even the same short Afro.

Breeze's mobile phone vibrates in his vest pocket. He pulls it out see the reminder. His tenure proposal review is in thirty minutes with Dr. Talbert. He needs composure, but he is being assaulted by an emotion, one so violating that he starts vomiting the up cheeseburger.

Knight and the little white girl step away as he empties the contents of his stomach onto their layout table. He slumps and cannot stop the heaves. He drops to his knees. Knight comes to assist him up into a chair.

"Are you ok, Breeze?"

He takes a breath.

"Yes, I think so. I haven't eaten meat in almost a year. I think the cheeseburger was too much for my system. My sincere apologies."

He attempts to stand, but his knees fail him, and he drops back down to the chair.

Breeze heard about the shooting this past weekend, but the news didn't mention a child, and the incident appeared justified from the initial reports. The suspect had a handgun.

"Stay seated," comes from Knight.

Breeze notices the little white girl is looking at him strangely, but he can't read her expression.

"Allow me to clean up my mess."

"No." Knight extends his hand and helps him up, "Let's get you some fresh air."

He walks Breeze up front and out the glass front door.

Breeze really hadn't eaten meat in over a year, but what assaulted him was the news report, not the meat. What trained police officer shoots a twelve-year-old?

Outside, he takes in the fresh air.

"Jeremy did say a twelve-year-old, didn't he?"

"Yeah, damn, that's what he said." Knight is looking at him intently. "If a cop dies tomorrow, my office kid is right, no? And she has a story."

Breeze already knows she has a story, which is unfortunate for her. He will have to report her to the APS because Knight will get behind her and the story. Her death may upset Knight enough to postpone or stop any investigation she may have begun. She is unaware how detrimental her snooping could be. Breeze knows there is a plan in motion, and nothing or no one will stop the wheels. Now, it will only be unfortunate for her, but if she is successful in involving the paper, it will be unfortunate for them all. She must be reported to stop the deaths of others.

Standing outside in front of the journal office, Breeze tells Knight, "I have to go man, a tenure meeting."

"You still fighting for it?"

"Yes. Dr. Talbert won't let me let it go. He is fighting for it more than I."

Knight smiles and says, "He wants his protégé in his seat."

"So it seems. I left you the names of the organizations and contact people that were able to stop school closings in other cities. I have spoken with all of them. You call them, then call me back, and we will start mapping our plan of action."

Knight nods his head agreeing.

"Cool. Did you include Banks and The Freedom Protesters?"

Breeze lowers his head; this day is not going well at all. Why is Banks even on Knight's mind?

"No, I didn't. They are not effective."

The mild winter has allowed Breeze to wear a three-piece suit with no overcoat. He looks down at his forest green suit, white shirt, and black tie to see if any vomit splattered on him. He sees none; however, his chest remains tight, and he is sweating.

A grimace has appeared on Knight's face. He obviously disagrees with Breeze's summation of Banks and his organization.

"What? You got him wrong, man. They got the High-bolt area schools to remain open. He is very effective."

"O.K. Well I didn't contact him, but that doesn't mean you can't."

From their past experience, Breeze knows it is pointless to argue with Knight. He always does what he wants despite group decisions. And besides, Breeze is certain that Banks and his organization are about to be nullified, but he doesn't want Knight caught in the crossfire.

"Yeah, I will give him a call."

Of course he will, Breeze thinks. It's just that type of day.

"You don't look well, Breeze."

"Who is well these days, brother? With our people, our children, being gunned down by police? No, I'm not well. I will call you in a couple of days about our next move against the school closings."

Breeze forces his legs to move; his muscles have stiffened with anger. He pulls his keys from his pocket and blinks the lights on his white Camry. He parked two stores down. He walks to the car without turning around to see if Knight remained outside.

Dr. Talbert's secretary, Melody, is also an assassin. She, like Breeze, had to go to school for her job, her cover job. She majored in sociology, and they had actually taken some undergraduate classes together. Dr. Talbert and the American Purist Society recruited her from the same state mental hospital as Breeze. However, her study didn't require a doctorate; Breeze's did, and he is grateful for the study but not the tenure pursuit.

Breeze hates jumping through the hoops Dr. Talbert deems necessary for secure cover. Melody knows he is an assassin, but she never speaks to him outside her cover. Her conversation with him has become all University based. Today, she has him sitting in the outer office waiting to see Dr. Talbert like any other professor in tenure review. Her light brown eyes are looking over her ivory horn-rimmed glasses to him.

"Give him about ten more minutes, Dr. Breeze. He's running a little late today. How did your consult go this morning?"

"It went well, thank you for the heads up."

"Don't thank me, Dr. Talbert had me send her to you. He was too busy for the consult."

He nods and smiles indicating that he understands. He assumed Melody sent the young reporter over to him since she was investigating the police killings; he was wrong. The student was referred because of Dr. Talbert's schedule.

Melody doesn't return his smile or offer any type of cheerful warmth. She is nine years younger than

Breeze. He knows her birthday is September fourth two days after his. Breeze is guessing that their shared history stops her from being cordial.

Twelve years ago, he sat in the dayroom of the psychiatric institution and watched her bang holes into plasterboard of the walls with her head. And once at dinner, she chewed another patient's eye out with her bottom teeth. But what Breeze thinks stops her from being friendly is her remembering fucking him for his tapioca Jell-O and chocolate milk. She demanded the two together.

At the mental institution, some female patients exchanged sexual favors for cigarettes, ice cream, bagels, chocolate milk, or a single serving of the rationed tapioca pudding. But with Melody, Breeze remembered that it had to be the two items together: two tapiocas alone didn't get him any of her pussy, neither would five chocolate milks, the combination had to be complete: tapioca pudding with chocolate milk. Patients only received tapioca pudding at lunch on Wednesdays, but chocolate milk was served every day. On tapioca Wednesdays, Melody and Breeze would fuck.

Breeze hasn't had sex in over five years, and he doesn't miss it, but whenever he sees Melody, he reminisces about the physical contact of the act. Not that sex with Melody was all that memorable, but she does make him think about having sex. He guesses that seeing him sparks the memory for her as well.

His anger over the child killed in Cleveland has subsided a great deal. The drive and sitting in the office before meeting with Dr. Talbert has calmed him down, and that is a good thing because he knows his anger is a red flag for Dr. Talbert, and Dr. Talbert taught him it should be a red flag for himself as well, but Breeze enjoys feeling anger . . . especially justified anger.

"He will see you now, Dr. Breeze."

Melody motions toward the closed door behind with her open hand. She avoids eye contact with him. Standing, he decides to bring her a six-pack of tapioca pudding with a quart of chocolate milk on his next visit. Perhaps that will elicit some civility. He pushes open Dr. Talbert's inner office door.

Entering the office, Breeze sees the lowered, totally gray head of the only man that offered him life guidance for the betterment of himself. Until he met Dr. Talbert, no man, Black or white had shown any interest or concern for him as a human being, not one. And the sad part was, he didn't know someone should have. He didn't expect what he was never given.

Breeze was one of the newborn babies found in an alley garbage can crying, and he has lived his life knowing that, so what he has expected from others was minimal. He never expected to be treated like someone's son, brother, nephew, or grandson; he was attached to no one, and he never forgets that he was found in an alley garbage can crying.

"Noble, I spent last evening reviewing your portfolio. You did a good job."

Dr. Talbert looks from the packet to Breeze.

"Your portfolio is ready. The revisions are on target. I will re-submit it to the committee chair this afternoon."

Breeze takes the seat in front of Dr. Talbert's oak desk and says, "Good deal, sir."

There was a time when the only address Breeze had for him was, "Fuck you white man," never "sir." That was when Dr. Talbert wore his neckties tied in Windsor knots with button collar white shirts. He doesn't wear ties now due to arthritis in his fingers.

"The road has been a bit longer than speculated, but we are on track. How many classes are you teaching this term?"

"I have six, with three independent studies."

"And your research?"

"The grant from the state and the American Purist Society is allowing it to continue. The first half of the paper will be published in the APA journal this spring."

"That's your third article with them, no?"

"Yes, sir, eight published in other academic journals last year, which includes two book reviews of your release."

Breeze smiles at him.

"Yes, well, it fared better under your prose than others."

Dr. Talbert returns Breeze's smile showing his top brownish incisor. All of his teeth are yellow, but the top brown one has attracted Breeze attention for decades. He has watched the tooth go from the dullest white one, to yellow, to dark yellow, to brown. The tooth has always been the darkest among all of Talbert's stained teeth.

Dr. Talbert leans back in the leather office chair and says, "Your APS assignment has ended. From their communications, the materials are in place, and the call to the police is being made as we speak."

The smile has left his narrow wrinkled face.

"Your work was stellar, Noble. The five kills only left evidence that we wanted left. "

His praise has meant everything to Breeze for over two decades. From his academic study, he is aware Dr. Talbert's praises started out as positive reinforcement to increase desired behavior, and it eventually transitioned into parental praise, which it remains for Breeze today.

"Is there a problem with ending the assignment?" Dr. Talbert queries.

"Not really, sir."

And there isn't, not really, Breeze thinks. With the assignment ending, there is no need to report the little white girl. The killings will stop, and her story will end.

With his eyes still on Breeze, Dr. Talbert says, "Banks and his organization should be on the evening news. The mission is accomplished. The guns have been placed and treated with his and three other member's fingerprints. Your shooting locations correlate with their known locations at the time of the shootings. I doubt the trials will last three months, and now the country will see Banks and his followers as the seditious troublemaking barbarians that they are. And you are ordered to cease and desist your school closing protest.

"The success of Banks' local movement is feeding into a national movement. Others are following his lead with some success, and the APS views a national movement as subversive. These school closings are part of a larger plan that is in motion, and the few successes of those blocking the closings across the country are delaying that plan."

Breeze knows that Dr. Talbert will not inform him of what the larger action is. He never does. Sometimes he can surmise a plan from the media. Over the years, he has learned how to follow APS breadcrumbs.

"The protest is linked to my research."

"Desist." Dr. Talbert says with finality.

"Yes, sir."

"Did you note the increase in your monthly APS stipend?"

He did, and Breeze was quite pleased with it.

"Yes, sir. It was duly noted."

"It was society-wide, not saying that you do not deserve an individual merit raise that is coming as well." Dr. Talbert begins rubbing his swollen arthritic right hand with his left, "You seem tense, Noble."

He doesn't lie to Dr. Talbert, so Breeze tells him, "There was a shooting in Ohio, and it has gotten under my skin. The police killed a child there this past weekend."

"Yes, in Cleveland. I know."

"And it angered me."

"Because the victim was a child?"

"Because he was another Afro-American child killed by a white police officer."

"Oh, I see. Would I be assuming correctly, if I say you were disappointed that the assignment ended?"

Dr. Talbert returns to rubbing his swollen knuckles.

"You would be correct."

Breeze makes the statement with no apprehension; there is no fear in their relationship, at least not of Dr. Talbert. He does fear the APS as a whole.

"Ok, Noble."

He looks up from his knuckles to Breeze.

"Allow me to remind that you are an APS agent, trained to keep the American homeland safe against all threats, foreign and domestic."

He stops rubbing his arthritic fingers.

Over the years, Breeze has learned Dr. Talbert's temperament from his facial expressions. There are no stress lines in his forehead presently; the tips of his ears are not turning red, neither his upper lip nor his left eye is twitching, and no condescending smile is present. His words are parental, not managerial.

"You recent assignment wasn't a social reckoning. You didn't assassinate those five white officers due to colored people being killed. You assassinated those officers to eliminate the threat of Renaldo Banks and his Freedom Protesters. We are not dealing in colored and white race issues, Noble.

"We are concerned with safety, American homeland safety. When you were your sickest, you killed to be an American. Yes, in your racially skewed mind you thought that meant you had to be white; but you have learned that being an a American is not about skin color. It is about a dedication to freedom, constant loyalty to this country, and a devotion to the laws of this land. That is what makes us patriots. I saw your patriotism in the killing of that little boy. That boy you skinned in that alley became a martyr. His death brought you to a greater good."

Dr. Talbert pauses with his eyes still on Breeze; he rarely mentions the killing that brought Breeze under his care.

"I was concerned that this assignment might cause you to de-focus and forget that you are beyond race, Noble. And so is this country, and so is the American Purist Society. What we do as agents for the APS is beyond race. People who are naïve enough to think that race matters are ignorant of the reality we live in. We use race as a tool, nothing more. People who believe race matters are those who will be upset about Banks and his organization killing white officers. Their support and outrage will allow us to neutralize the threat he and his organization have become. He and his organization are disrupting the status quo, and that is the problem. It has nothing to do with him being colored. The goal, the end result of your assignment, is not racially motivated. The end result is for the safety of the country, which I am certain you understand."

And Breeze does understand, Dr. Talbert is correct. His mind had de-focused. The police killing so many

43

Black people had disrupted his thinking. He was thinking like the masses of Afro-Americans, and getting upset as if race mattered. Dr. Talbert and the APS have taught him that race is a tool, nothing more. His anger was a result of being de-focused. He had begun to think that he was killing in response to the police shootings, and it happened so subtly. Dr. Talbert is correct. He has been trained to think beyond race. His assignments, his actions, are for the betterment of America, not the Black race. He is an American who happens to be Black. He knows this. He has learned this. His actions, the police killings, were part of a larger plan, not a reckoning of a supposed injustice against Afro-Americans.

He exhales deeply and looks up at the man who pulled him from the mire of sick, delusional thinking that was his life for so long, and he tells him, "I had de-focused, sir."

"Yes, I suspected you might. It was a difficult assignment, but we were certain you would complete it, and you have. The death of that child in Cleveland is unfortunate, and the sad truth is many more children may die for the betterment of this country, but we must stay on task. We cannot afford to flounder in our thinking or our actions. There is too much work to be done. Too many threats to the American way of life exist. Subversives are materializing daily. Banks and his Freedom Protesters are not alone in disrupting America and in their desire to bring this country to its knees. There are legions of others, and it is only patriots like us who stop them in their tracks."

Chapter Five

Jeremy filled a bucket full of soapy water and rags and has begun cleaning off the layout table. To help him, Denise fills up the mop bucket and began mopping up Dr. Breeze's vomit from under and around the table.

Jeremy says, "The squad car hadn't even stopped before the cop got out with his gun gun blazing. He shot that poor kid without saying a word. He didn't wait to see if he was armed or anything. No warning, nothing, he just shot him down. Wait until you see it. Honestly, it makes me want to do something. Drive to Cleveland and protest or something."

He has stopped wiping the layout table and is just standing there staring at the clean table. Denise keeps mopping and looking at him gazing at the cleaned table. She and Jeremy moved in together during the spring semester. He had a place off-campus, and she was in the dorms, but once they started dating seriously she moved in with him. From living with him, she has learned that when he stops talking, he's thinking. Which is weird to her, because she thinks better when she is talking.

"What this means, this shooting in Cleveland, means that tonight or tomorrow . . . a white cop is going to die," is what Jeremy says to the clean spot on the table.

"What did you say?"

Denise stops mopping. She heard him, but she wants him to say it again.

He drops the rag into the bucket.

"You heard me, and you know like I know. Damn. I don't want to see an innocent person die, but damn . . . I won't be mad if another white cop gets shot."

She rests the mop handle against the table.

"What did you say?"

She couldn't have heard him right.

"I'm tired of it being Black people always dying. I know wishing any person's death is not right, but I am tired of it being Blacks all the time. I feel like hunting season is open and Blacks are the game. Cops, white cops, are shooting us when they fucking feel like it. So, yeah . . . I want a white cop to die."

The Jeremy she loves doesn't talk like this. He has never said such hateful words, such racially charged words. He always, always goes for the middle ground trying to see both sides fairly.

"That is anger speaking, Jeremy. Not you."

She is trying to look into his downcast eyes.

He looks up at her.

"It's not anger. It's disgust, disgust in this system. What was that cop thinking?"

"I found it!" Mildred yelled, "It's right here on YouTube, come on y'all."

Mildred turns her computer screen, so they all can see it. Denise is almost afraid to watch. If it angered Jeremy so, it is sure to upset her, and her emotions last for weeks, for months at a time, and they can lead to long depressions. Jeremy is aware of this.

"Should I watch?" She asks him.

Tears are welling in his eyes.

"It's going to hurt, a lot."

He kisses her on the forehead. She stands next to her boyfriend and watches the video.

"Damn," comes from Mr. Knight. He is standing behind them.

Mildred says, "Oh my god, that ain't right. How long did they let him lay there unattended? Not one of those bastards checked to see if he was alive? Where is the ambulance? Did they even call for an ambulance? This is some bullshit. What the fuck!"

Mildred gets up from her desk and walks away from the screen to the front door. She stands at the door and starts crying.

"What, when, damn! Is it ever going to stop? When will they start treating us like people? When?"

Denise feels her own tears. He was a kid playing in the park. Where kids are supposed to play. Jeremy was right, no way was any warning given. She doubts that the police even saw a gun. When she first opens her mouth to speak, she can't. Jeremy puts his arm around her. To him, she finally says, "They just shot him and left him there bleeding. Why on earth did they shoot him? Why?"

No one answers. She looks into each face, Jeremy, and Mr. Knight's, and neither answers.

"Because we ain't people to them," Mildred moans from the door. "We ain't shit to them. We don't fucking matter. You're right, Jeremy; I hope a fucking white cop dies tonight. I hope whoever is killing them finds one and blows his fucking brains all over the street. I got to go, Mr. Knight. I got to go home and check on my boys. I got to go."

And she opens the glass door and leaves.

Denise has never consciously felt different than the others in the office before. She feels different right now even with her boyfriend's arm around her, and she feels guilty of something because she is white. She feels guilty because she doesn't want an innocent cop to die, to get murdered. Yes, she is sad for the boy, but two wrongs don't make a right. Those police officers have families, too; they are someone's sons, too.

Mr. Knight sits in the chair Mildred left empty and backs up the video. Denise can't watch it again.

"I have to go," she tells Jeremy.

"Go, I understand," he says in her ear. "I'll meet you at home later."

He releases her from the supportive hug and pulls the chair from their desk to sit with his dad.

Denise feels like an outsider, and she has never felt this way before, not with Jeremy and not at the paper. She should stay, but she can't watch it again, and she doesn't want to hear Jeremy wish for another man's death. She should go, but she doesn't leave and starts watching the video again.

The boy posed no threat to the officers. He was walking toward the squad car, not running away. She leaves before he is shot.

At home, sitting on their futon, she can't stop herself from powering on her laptop and searching for the shooting. The boy's name was Tamir Rice, and the original police report is totally different from the video. Tamir didn't have a gun in his hand, and no warning was given. Why did the officer shoot? She hears Mildred's answer repeating in her mind, "Because we ain't people to them." She turns the computer off stretches out on the futon and sleeps.

It was the turning of newspaper pages that woke her. Her first class isn't until 1:30 on Tuesdays. They sleep in on Tuesdays, but this morning Denise hears Jeremy groaning. The clock reads 4:45; it's still dark outside. Either he didn't sleep or he woke up early and ran four blocks to the 24-hour drugstore for the paper.

One thing is certain. He did run because she smells his perspiration.

Some news from the Internet must have spurred him out of the apartment for the paper. It is not a distrust of Internet news; it is a validation of facts that sends them to the daily papers. Wiping the sleep from her eyes, she sits up in the futon to see him rifling through both city papers. One headline reads, 'Three Officers Killed.'

"No!" she says, almost screaming. The other headline reads, 'Three Dead Policeman, City in Shock.' "No!" she throws back the sheet and crawls to the paper Jeremy isn't reading.

"I got stopped twice going to get the papers this morning, and I was on foot. Imagine how hard it's going to be to drive. I betcha they are going to establish roadblocks even without a suspect descriptions. This city is about to lose it."

"Oh, my God."

She is looking at the photos in the paper; two of the three policemen look like high-school kids.

"It looks like the shootings started two hours after the video was released. The first one happened at a traffic light; the officer was the driver, and a man just ran up to the squad car and shot him and kept running. The second officer was on the precinct steps about to report for work when a van drove by and opened fire; he was shot fifteen times, and they don't even know the color of the van. The third police officer was at a burger drive-thru when two assailants opened up on him and his partner. His partner is in critical condition with three gun shot wounds to the chest. This is worse than anyone could have predicted. What I said out of anger was not to materialize – not like this. God, not like this. They are going to turn the city into a war zone."

"Who?" She asks Jeremy still reading the article.

"The police: the city police, the state police, the National Guard, and the military. This cannot stay a Falcon City police matter. The whole country will respond to this. It was the state police that stopped me on the way home. This article is calling for the National Guard already."

Looking up from the article, she says, "Well, I think it's needed. Maybe Falcon City police will be too emotionally attached to police the incident."

"Every white law officer and military personnel sent here will be emotionally attached to these shootings. Nothing good will come from more boots on the ground. What they are proposing will not stop police from being shot or stop the police from shooting others. The last thing this city needs is more police."

He is looking at her as if she is a child who doesn't understand that one plus one equals two. She is about to tell him that this article is calling for the National Guard too, but she doesn't because she agrees with the article; four officers shot and three killed is a state of emergency, and the National Guard should be called.

"Well, what do you think should happen?"

His arm drops and the paper spreads out on the carpet.

"I don't know, but this," he points to the paper, "more police, isn't it. Maybe addressing the issue of improper policing, put the light on that issue . . . racism within this country's policing policy."

"But officers are being shot down, immediate action is required."

"So are citizens. Blood is being spilt on both sides."

"Sides? What sides? The police and citizens are on the same side. The police work for us."

"No, the police work to protect the state, not the citizens."

"Only some police. In general, the police serve and protect."

"They didn't protect Tamir Rice. They are not protecting me."

"But they are protecting you. Yes, there are some improprieties, but Jeremy, we need the police. There would be chaos without police."

"What do you think we have now?"

"We have a problem, not chaos. There exists a rule of law, and it must be maintained."

"At what cost, and why? Why maintain a system that is killing those it is supposed to protect?"

"You are being extreme. What would you replace police with? Society needs martialing."

Before he can answer her again, they hear rapid gunfire outside their window.

Jeremy gets up from the futon and goes to light switch on the wall and flips it off darkening the room.

"Stay down," he tells Denise, and drops to his knees and crawls to the window. He is peeping through the bottom half of the window.

More rapid shots are fired lighting up the dark room. The rapid shots are followed by single blasts. More rapid shots and a voice over a loudspeaker demands, "Drop your weapon."

"Fuck you!" is the screamed reply followed by more single shots.

The rapid shots are coming from more than one source and they are continuous. Spots of light are popping up all through their dark room. The rapid gunfire is nonstop until they hear an explosion that almost shatters their small living room window. Jeremy lies flat on the floor.

"Damn!" he screams.

Denise is too scared to move. She didn't lay down. She is still sitting on the futon with the newspaper in her lap. The light of flames is dancing on their walls. Jeremy rises up to the peep out of the window.

"Fuck, they shot up a Bonneville. Wait, it's Clinton's car. Damn, that is Clinton's car on fire. And Lord have mercy, Clinton is getting out of the car on fire."

Jeremy gets up and runs out of the door.

She screams, "No!"

Chapter Six

Dr. Noble Breeze watches his phone ringing. On the third ring, he picks it up without speaking. He hasn't slept the entire night. He couldn't, with the police monitor reporting the shootings. He was in bed, and police officers were dying, and not by his hands.

"I guess we were wrong, huh?"

He recognizes Knight's voice.

"Perhaps."

"They are doing it, Breeze. Our people are fighting back."

"You don't know that Blacks shot those officers."

Knight's assumptions have always irritated Breeze since undergrad.

"Come on, man. All of Falcon City knows that Black people are shooting at police. Have you looked out your window? Oh, that's right, you live around white people. Well, in Black neighborhoods the police are everywhere. I see a squad car every thirty seconds, and have you heard about Banks and The Freedom Protesters? They were the first to snap. I don't know why, but Falcon City SWAT surrounded their building, and before the police could deploy from their trucks, Banks and his followers opened fire on them. The three SWAT trucks had to drive away."

"Yes, but they voluntarily turned themselves in twenty minutes later."

"Yep, and that was smart. Now everybody knows that they are in police custody, and that they walked into that station alive, which would not have been the case had SWAT entered their headquarters."

"That could be true."

Breeze is certain it is true. The APS wants Banks and his followers dead.

"Oh, I got to let you go. My son is calling. He probably wants to gloat about his little girlfriend being right. Talk to you, man."

Breeze places the phone back in the cradle.

She wasn't right, he thinks, but he was wrong; Afro-Americans are killing police. He stands from the bed still dressed in his three-piece suit and black wingtips. He laid down to rest for a minute, but once he clicked on the police monitor he didn't move.

His neighborhood isn't white, but it is upscale and mostly white people do live in the area. He brought the two-bedroom condominium when City University hired him as an assistant professor. Since he hasn't looked out the window, he walks from his bedroom to the living room, which has glass patio doors that give him a street view.

He stands at the patio doors for five minutes and doesn't see one police car. He sees no traffic. He opens the glass door and steps out onto the patio. There is a small amount of bluish light from the rising sun; the color of the sky matches dusk, but his neighbor's ringing alarm clock signifies dawn. His neighbor doesn't have a patio, and Breeze guesses the east-facing window is in her bedroom. The alarm is silenced.

Breeze notices a police car has stopped beneath his patio. The squad car's search lamp is switched on. Breeze watches the light beam quickly advance from the street to the sidewalk, to his building, and up the building to his seventh floor patio where it surrounds him. He consciously doesn't step back and out of the light. He looks down at the police car despite the painful bright light in his eyes. The light is switched off, and the squad car drives away. Breeze blinks his eyes to readjust them to the dawn.

"Yes, it is obvious that I belong here."

He turns and takes steps through patio doors. The living room area of the condominium is still furnished with demo furniture because he brought condominium model and made a deal for the all furniture. The only things he has added are bath towels, sheets, dishes, a coffee maker, pots and pans, bookcases, a laptop, the police monitor, and a television he has yet to cut on.

Standing with his back to the patio doors looking at the black screen of wall-mounted television, he hears the coffee maker beep and start brewing. It is 5:00 am. He looks at the television and thinks about the local news, and then he looks to the counter that divides the living area from the kitchen and sees his laptop. He decides on the Internet news. He exhales deeply and walks to the laptop.

When he opens it, email notifications are blinking on the screen. He pats his suit jacket and removes his phone. He sees three missed calls and three missed text messages. The emails, calls, and text messages are all from Dr. Talbert. When Breeze focuses, as he did while listening to the police monitor, he misses calls and text. He dials Dr. Talbert's number.

Dr. Talbert doesn't answer with a greeting.

"We have a meeting at seven with the President. He is staying at the Falcon City Hotel on Michigan. Meet you in the lobby at ten to the hour."

Dr. Talbert hangs up after directives.

Breeze walks back to the patio door windows. APS meetings have never been reactionary in the past. The meetings are always planning. Now they are meeting in response to an action not to prevent or manipulate. He smiles thinking about Knight – "Our people are fighting back."

Chapter Seven

Denise covers her nightshirt with Jeremy's robe and runs after him in her bare feet. When she breaks the door front of their apartment building, she sees a line of police with rifles pointing at her building. Jeremy is ten paces ahead of her. His hands are up, but he is screaming for Clinton who is on his knees aflame next to the burning Bonneville. Despite the police orders to stop, Jeremy continues to Clinton.

She yells to Jeremy to stop, but he doesn't. The rapid-fire of police rifles stop him. Denise stops in mid-step. She watches Jeremy take backward steps. The police fire again and Jeremy is knocked on his back by a barrage of police bullets.

Denise can't move.

She sees Jeremy bleeding and twitching on the sidewalk. Her shoulder and thigh are burning. She looks down and sees her robe and legs are bloody.

"Jeremy," she screams and collapses to the sidewalk crawling towards him.

"Stop firing," she hears when she reaches Jeremy.

There are bloody holes and spots covering his face and his chest. She grabs him and pulls him to her. The butt of a rifle breaks her embrace. She reaches for him again, but she is kicked in the face.

"Lay still, bitch," is the order given from the boots that kicked her in the face. Boots surround her. Some of them kick Jeremy, and others stomp out the flame that was Clinton. Stomp out.

Jeremy is dragged to the curb like a garbage bag. She wants to yell out, but she is unable, something heavy is on her chest, but she can't see what it is. Smoke is in her eyes, and she can't breathe. A light is flashed in her eyes, and fingers are on her neck and in her mouth. Her eyes are forced open and again a light is in them. A mask is placed over her nose, and she is able to breathe. She is lifted from the sidewalk and carried to an ambulance by police officers.

They get her to the ambulance toss her in and leave. In Jeremy's robe pocket, she feels his phone. His father's number is on the screen. She pushes the number and rips the mask off.

"They killed him. They killed Jeremy!"

It is all she can say before she passes out on the floor of the ambulance.

When she wakes, she is strapped down on a stretcher still in the back of the ambulance. Across from her is a police officer who is also strapped down on stretcher. The phone is under a strap on her chest. She can see her thigh is bandaged. She passes out again.

Denise Thomson wakes in a room full of people on hospital gurneys. The other patients look like soldiers and police. She tries to sit up, but she is still strapped down. "Jeremy," she calls out, "Jeremy!" she yells through the oxygen masks.

"The Jane Doe is awake," she hears.

A man dressed in blue scrubs comes to her.

"What's your name?"

"Is Jeremy here?"

The man repeats, "What is your name?" while taking off her mask.

"Denise Thomson, my name is Denise Thomson. My fiancé, Jeremy Knight, is he here?"

She is hopeful, but she remembers the police dragging him to the curb.

"I don't know, Ms. Thomson. You are in the county hospital. You were shot in the thigh and shoulder during a riot. You have to remain calm and as motionless as possible. We don't want to open your sutured wounds. Please be still. The doctor will be with you shortly."

A riot, she thinks.

"What riot?"

"Lay still, Ms. Thomson."

And he walks away.

"My parents," she says to his back.

"Jeremy," she says to no one, but hears, "He's gone."

She turns her head and sees Mr. Knight standing to her right.

"I came as soon as you called. I got there minutes after you called. He was already dead on the curb. They shot him to death, and wouldn't let me touch him. They kept him out there on the street until the morgue wagon came and hauled him and others away. I tried to tell them I was his father, but they drew their guns on me and told me to step away. I watched them put him in a bag. It was liked you said, they killed him."

Mr. Knight placed a book bag on her gurney by her feet.

"After they left, I went into his apartment and got your purse and something for you to wear. Did you know his mother died giving him life? It was only me and him. Me and my son, and they killed him, just like you said. They killed my beautiful son."

He exhaled with such force that his breath shock tears from Denise's eyes. She wept watching him leave the emergency ward.

"He should have stopped," she softly cried. "He should have stopped when the police told him to. They told him to stop. I told him to stop, but he didn't, and they shot him. They shot him. He should have stopped."

She wanted to roll over and bury her face in the pillow and cry, but she is strapped down to the gurney.

63

Chapter Eight

Breeze decided to dress in his first tailor-made suit for the meeting. When APS sent his bonus, he decided to purchase the suit. It was made with blue wool of the highest quality with a finish that shone. He stood looking down at the suit on his bed. Never did imagine owning such clothing. Even after he earned his Ph.D., he thought such dress was for rich businessmen. He bought the suit simply because he could afford it. Along with the suit, he purchased a dozen custom white shirts with button-down collars similar to the ones Dr. Talbert wore.

After his shower and dressing for the meeting, he gets into a celebratory mood. He isn't sure why, but he feels as if celebration is in order; thus, the tailored suit. He showers with the police monitor playing in the background. He doesn't give the reports his total attention as he did done the night before, but he hears the announcements. He hears the protest, the revolts, and the discontent of the Blacks in Falcon City. They are letting the country know that they have had enough.

Once dressed, he pulls his firearm case from beneath the bed. These pistols are his, not the throwaways given to him for APS assignments. These are pistols he values. His work with APS is secret, so he is not granted a permit to carry through the

Society, but as a private citizen with no felony arrest or arrest. Due to his life created by Dr. Talbert and the APS, he was able to receive a license to carry. From his collection, he chooses the Desert Eagle .9mm. He holsters the pistol in the small of his back under his suit vest. He slips into the jacket and gives himself a once-over in the tall mirror. He likes what he sees and exits his condominium.

He doesn't drive four blocks before he sees police squad car lights in his rearview mirror. He sees two white officers in the squad car, and they are pulling him over. He drives through the intersection and pulls over in a bus stop on the avenue. The traffic is consistent with any other Tuesday morning at six-thirty a.m., workers driving to work.

He puts his Camry in park and places both hands on the steering wheel. Both officers exit the squad. One approaches the passenger side; the other approaches him on the driver's side. Breeze has all four windows down in the sedan.

"Good morning, bro. License and registration, please?" The white officer asks.

Breeze hears the 'bro' greeting but doesn't respond. He pulls his wallet from inside his jacket and hands the officer at the window his license.

"I will need to reach into the glove box for the registration," he informs the officer.

"Go ahead, brother."

He retrieves the registration and hands it to the same officer.

"What's your business in the area?"

"I live half a mile west of here. I am on my way to a meeting."

"What type of work do you do?"

"I teach at City University."

"Oh, an educated brother, huh?"

"Sorry?"

"A teacher, so you must have an education?"

"Yes, I have a degree."

"Are you aware that martial law has been established in the city?"

"No, I wasn't, but I am sure if city officials deemed it necessary, it must be."

"Yeah, it appears that the brothers are shooting police."

Breeze hears the goading in the officer's words and tone.

"You didn't get the message, bro?" The officer asks smiling.

"May I ask why you stopped me, officer?"

"You can ask whatever you want," the officer at the passenger window says.

"I'm going to need you step out of the car, Mr. Breeze," the officer at the driver's window says.

"Dr. Breeze," Breeze answers.

"What did you say?" The officer asks, stepping back and drawing his weapon.

Breeze calculates it will take a second to swing his door open far enough to strike the officer at the driver's window, and another second to free the thumb lock and draw his pistol and put two in the chest of the officer at the passenger window who hasn't drawn his weapon.

While reaching for his door handle, another squad car pulls up. A Black officer is driving the squad car alone.

"Damn, it's the Sergeant Brother Man," the officer at the passenger window exclaims.

The officer at the driver's window holsters his pistol and tosses Breeze's license and registration back through the window.

"Pull off, now," he orders.

Breeze puts his Camry in drive and complies, grinning. He nods his head at the Afro-American sergeant as he pulls into traffic. Even though grinning, Breeze is concerned with his thinking. He was ready to kill both officers, and that is a problem. Something is wrong in his mind. His thinking isn't quite right. It started with the celebratory mood. The city is in turmoil, and where is the cause for celebration in that?

No answer forms in his mind. Instead, he thinks about the police.

Breeze wishes the Black sergeant hadn't shown up because he wanted the conflict. He was more than ready to kill the white officers. He is not thinking like an APS agent, and that is a problem.

At the Falcon City Hotel, the police presence is invasive. Everywhere Breeze looks he sees armed men in uniform. Handing the valet his keys, he notices that the uniformed officers are looking but not looking at him. He receives several quick and sideways glances. He enters the hotel with his head held high ignoring the almost-looks. Perhaps he is being over-sensitive to the situation, he thinks.

When he enters the lobby, he spots Dr. Talbert and Melody standing in the elevator bank. Melody's legs have gotten Breeze's attention. She has on a blue skirt, which is barely above her nylon-covered knees. Her pink heels match her pink blouse, and Breeze wonders, is it the shoes that are causing him to look at her legs?

He approaches them with a "Good morning" and a smile. Dr. Talbert returns the smile. He receives a grunt from Melody.

"Good, we are a couple of minutes early. Let's go up," Dr. Talbert says pushing a call button. The elevator doors in front of him open immediately. On the elevator, Dr. Talbert presses the number twenty-four. They are the only ones on the car.

"Nice suit, Noble," Dr. Talbert compliments.

"Thank you, sir."

"Kind of shiny, for a professor, no?" Melody comments.

"I like it," Breeze answers looking her in the eye. She looks away.

The doors open on twenty-four, and they exit into a conference room.

There are about a hundred people sitting in chairs in front of a podium. At the podium is President Nelson, a thin man with a runner's build. He was an Olympic finalist in the nineties bringing home a bronze medal for the 100-meter run. Breeze remembers watching him run. He guesses that the President is in his forties. His hair remains intact, but he is beginning to gray at the temples.

"I guess we are not as early as I thought."

Dr. Talbert leads Melody and Breeze to the third row of seats and they sit. Surveying the room, Breeze notices there are no armed police present in the conference room. He was expecting a small meeting, not a small conference. The screen behind Nelson has a map of Falcon City schools with the schools in Black and Latino neighborhoods highlighted in blue. Breeze is familiar with the map.

"Education," President Nelson begins, "is the biggest threat to our American way of life. The past decades have shown that nothing brings unrest to the status quo as quickly as an educated mass."

The mumblings, greetings, and light conversations in the room are nearly silenced with his statement.

"For the past two decades, we have been successful on the state level with moving college education further away from the grasp of the masses, through tuition increases and state legislation that defunds public education. However, our efforts have been met with difficulties as of late, with grassroots organizations challenging our legislation.

"As long as these grassroots organization continue to challenge our established legislation and our proposed legislation on the state and federal levels, our efforts are hindered. To stop the education of the masses, which is the threat, we must continue to decrease state and federal funding to education. To decrease the funding, we must create another need for the funds. We have done this in the recent past by redirecting funds to the war on drugs, which translates to the funds being spent on policing as opposed to education. Americans, true Americans, want to feel safe. We faced little opposition in redirecting the funds in the past; however, the war on drugs is decreasing in importance in the minds of

Americans. Being tough on crime has led to more arrests of true Americans than predicted. This is not to say that our plan of increasing the funding of police is in error. However, we need to change the reason for funding the police.

"True Americans are no longer afraid of Mexican drug cartels invading suburban streets or Jamaican posses recruiting high school kids, but they are afraid of non-whites taking over. They are afraid of Muslims killing Christians. They are afraid of the white race becoming brown, and they are afraid of non-whites controlling the politics and economics of this country. To stop these changes, true Americans are willing to fund their police.

"They have supported legislation for homeland security, the NSA, and the militarization of local police. They feel comfort with heavily armed police, police in Humvees, police in bulletproof vest and helmets, and a stronger police presence. All of this comfort requires funding, and the funding comes when the need is apparent. Last night, Falcon City made the need apparent for many.

"True Americans will see grassroots organization like Banks and his Freedom Protestors as the homegrown terrorists that they are. When they opened fire on Falcon City SWAT, the whole country saw them as subversives."

The small congregation broke out in applause.

President Nelson calmed the group with waves of his hand, "But the war is not won with simple exposure. We must attack what they are doing. Their efforts, their message, must be belittled in the mind of the public. Yes, true Americans see these groups as troublemakers and rabble-rousers, but their actions, their grassroots campaigns, align others with their erroneous beliefs. All across this country, groups are fighting to stop school closings, to keep schools open that are draining funds from a greater need, a need for police. Police are needed to maintain the status quo, to keep America as it always was and as is shall remain, a country for true Americans."

The group of a hundred plus people applauds again in response.

When they settle, President Nelson continues with, "Understand this, educating the masses is a threat to the American Purist Society, and we see education of the masses as a threat to American life, and we will do everything in our power to make sure that only those worthy Americans will be educated in this country, people who know that this is God's country, and we are God's chosen people."

There is no settling the congregation. People are standing and applauding. President Nelson steps from around the podium and walks over to Dr. Talbert.

"We need to meet directly after."

He walks to a seat in the front row, and a Black man with locks takes the podium.

Breeze knows the man as Brother Jackson, one of the committee members on the school closing campaign that Knight organized.

"Thank you, President Nelson, for your words of guidance and purpose."

The crowd applauds again briefly.

"What you see on the overhead is a listing of Falcon City elementary schools and high schools. The schools highlighted in blue are the schools the city has marked for closing in the next three years."

Pausing the on-screen cursor over the High-bolt elementary school he says,

"This is the school targeted by a group forming on the south side of Falcon City. They are strategizing along the same lines as Banks and his Freedom Protestors involving the parents, churches, community centers, and some teachers. To date, the group has not contacted Banks, but it was inevitable due to Banks' success with another High-bolt school closing. Fortunately, his tutelage is no longer available," he says with a smirk.

Breeze smiles too, because it was his execution of APS assignments that led to Banks' arrest. Listening to

Brother Jackson, Breeze wonders whether he is an agent or merely a member of APS.

"The forming committee has been infiltrated by APS, so we are not expecting them to cohere into a threat. There are other committees forming in the Dillon Park and Bedford areas, and they are under surveillance by APS, Falcon City police, and the city administration, with whom we are working closely. Rest assured that APS goals are paramount for this city."

He ends his presentation with the applause of those in attendance. Breeze looks to Melody, who is not clapping or smiling. She returns his gaze and grunts. He, Jackson, and she are the only people of color at the small conference.

As people are standing to leave, Dr. Talbert tells them, "Remain seated," and leaves to greet the leaders in the front row.

"Are you buying all this?" Melody asks Breeze.

"All of what?" he answers with his eyes on Dr. Talbert.

"All of this true American propaganda?"

"They pay me, and as a dedicated employee, I support the Society's aims," is Breeze's answer.

"Yeah, but "true American" is another way of saying "white American.""

"No, they mean true Americans, patriots."

"Are you a patriot?"

He moves his gaze from Dr. Talbert to her.

"Yes, I am." He nods.

"Oh, since you are not white, at least you can be a patriot, huh?"

She crosses her legs at the knees and Breeze looks down, and again he is admiring her shapely nylon-covered legs.

He shakes his head in the negative, "No, dear, it's not about race; it's about loving this country."

He gives her the answer Dr. Talbert has given him dozens of times.

"You love this country?" She asks with her mouth twisted, "Then you buy it, huh?"

Breeze hears concern in the questions, something he hasn't heard in her words in quite a while. Their conversations have become very much matter-of-fact, procedural, a secretary scheduling for her boss, but there was a time when her words meant more to him. He looks at her intently.

Physically, he can't deny his attraction to her even with her mouth twisted. She has always turned him on sexually. Her light complexion with her strong African features excited him in the mental institution, and looking at her now they continue to excite him.

"Yes, I love this country. Don't you?"

She adjusts herself in the folding chair, uncrossing her legs, and sitting up straighter.

"I don't know. I certainly can't answer with your certainty."

"Few people can," he says with smile.

"You have gotten cocky, Dr. Breeze," she returns his smile.

"No, it's the new suit, not me."

"Ok, the suit. Noble . . . do you ever think about leaving?"

"What? The University? The city? The country?"

"No, well, yeah, maybe, but I was asking about the APS. Do you ever think about walking away from them?"

"How can I? They made me."

"Yes, I know," and she looks down from their shared contact, "but what they made, can change." She says looking up to him again, and Breeze sees her looking at him and not just on the surface. She is looking past him sitting in the conference, and her look sends him back: back to them watching Jeopardy in the dayroom of the institution, back to them standing in line for medication and him watching her pretend to take the medicine, back to them riding the institution's bus to the park, and back to tapioca pudding and chocolate milk.

"Are you dating, Noble?"

"No," he answers appreciating her looking at him.

"Why not, you got a new shiny suit?" She grins.

Before he can answer her, a fire alarm sounds and armed police pile out the elevator.

"We must evacuate, now!" is their shouted order.

There are more police in the room than remaining conference guests. Breeze hates being ordered, but he stands with Melody, and they follow behind an officer to the emergency door stairs.

President Nelson asks the police, "What's going on?"

"There was a demonstration on the street in front of the hotel. It moved to the lobby. Shots were fired. We are evacuating all guests. Please follow the officers down."

Breeze doubts Dr. Talbert's arthritis will allow him to walk down twenty-four flights of stairs.

He asks an officer, "Sir, Dr. Talbert" Breeze extends his hand toward Dr. Talbert, "will be unable to walk down twenty-four flight of stairs. Is the elevator available?"

"No, sir, there are being cut off due to protocol."

"Can we hurry to one?" Breeze asks.

"Sir, our orders are to evacuate all guests using the emergency stairs."

"But he has arthritis," Breeze darts at the officer.

"What if I refuse?" Dr. Talbert asks.

"Sir, I have my orders," the officer says watching the others exit.

"And I have arthritis. I cannot walk down twenty-four flights of stairs. I am physically unable."

"You stay here at your own risk, sir; shots have been fired within the hotel. Understand?" The officer's gaze is brief.

"I do, officer, and I chose to stay."

"I am staying with him, sir," Breeze announces.

"And so I'm I," Melody joins.

"Fine." The officer walks to the emergency stairs doorway.

President Nelson and the few others follow the police through the exit doors.

When they are through the doors and in the stairwell, Melody says, "I am going to check the elevator."

"Good idea," Dr. Talbert says and slowly follows her.

Melody moves quickly ahead. She is at the elevator call button before Dr. Talbert and Breeze.

The chime sounds and the red arrow lights up pointing down.

"I got one," she says with a smile.

They all board when the doors open. Again only the three are on the car.

"Let's hope we make it down." Dr. Talbert pushes the lobby button and the doors close.

In a matter of seconds, the elevator doors open to the lobby, and Dr. Talbert gasps, but neither Breeze nor Melody make a sound.

Black youth are running through the lobby, and they are literally running over bodies. Both police officers and civilians are spread bloody across the lobby's high-gloss white tile floors. The wounded are moaning and crying out, and the smell of gasoline and gunpowder are ripe in the air. Youth are disarming wounded and dead police officers, stripping them of their bulletproof vests and side arms.

The glass front of the hotel's gift shop is shattered by a youth with a police baton. The shop is ransacked in matter of seconds. There are no hotel staff or police protecting the establishment.

Breeze draws his pistol from the small of his back, and Melody retrieves hers from her red purse.

Dr. Talbert is hesitant to step from the elevator bay.

"Slowly," Breezes says to him, "slowly walk in front us."

They step into the melee.

Breeze is on Dr. Talbert's left and Melody is on his right. They have to step over a white man in a suit gurgling his own blood. Neither of them reaches down to help the wounded man. They proceed with caution amidst a violent crowd toward the shattered glass lobby doors. There is no barrier between them and the street. The bronzed lobby glass is splintered into thousands of bits that crunch with each step they take. They are steps away from outside.

"Where the fuck you going, white man?" asks a man entering the hotel through the frame that once held the glass front. He is pointing a shotgun at Dr. Talbert.

Breeze doesn't hesitate to rock the man's head back with two rounds. The man drops to his knees and falls backwards. The shotgun falls to his side, and it is immediately picked up by a running youth who blazes past them. Breeze sees his Camry parked behind a gold Porsche. There are six other cars in the valet spots. He looks to valet desk and sees kids rifling through the keys. The Porsche is the first to go.

Breeze slightly pushes Dr. Talbert towards the Camry. A black Dodge Charger peels from its valet park. Breeze sees his Camry keys in a boy's hand. The boy is running from the desk to the Camry.

"He has my keys," he says to Melody, who he surmises has a better shot. She fires one shot that forces the boy's leg to an angle that allows gravity to yank him to the blacktop of the driveway.

When they get to the Camry, Breeze takes the keys from the crying boy's hand. He unlocks all the doors and opens the back door for Dr. Talbert.

"Motherfuckers!" the crying boy yells, "Hey, these cops are trying to leave!"

Dr. Talbert gets in and Breeze closes the back door.

He sees the crowd at the valet desk looking in their direction. He looks to Melody on the passenger side. She is already in a marksman stance and fires six rounds. The crowd at the valet desk is no more.

Inside the car, Breeze thinks about backing up over the screaming kid, but he doesn't. He pulls from the hotel blacktop onto Michigan Avenue.

"Thank you, Jesus!" Dr. Talbert exclaims.

Either Breeze or Melody comment, their eyes are on the approaching SWAT units.

"Four," she counts.

"Too much, too late," is Breeze's answer as he passes the SWAT vans.

Chapter Nine

"They are not going to admit you. The doctor is sure your sutures will hold, and I am happy with that decision. This hospital isn't known for competent patient care," her father says pushing his glasses back up the bridge of his nose. He is wearing the white *City University Dad* t-shirt she got him for Father's Day.

"Perhaps it isn't, but she was shot, and they should at least keep her overnight. Releasing her is ludicrous. Who gets shot twice, and released the same day? But I agree with your father, getting you away from these people is best," her mother says without whispering as her father did. She pulls strands of brunette hair from her forehead and blue eyes.

When her mother says "these people," Denise knows she is talking about the Black nurses and doctor in the emergency room. She doesn't think of her mother as hateful or prejudiced, just class-conscious and ignorant of the fact that her class statements come off as racist when the class she views as beneath her is a minority class. She is ignorant, if not totally oblivious, to the fact that minorities are often above her in class and wealth. Her mother assumes that white people are always superior.

Even though they are nowhere close to sharing a worldview or seeing the inequalities in the country, they do have the same eyes. Their eyes are the same in color, shape, depth, and her father says they have same ability to pierce, but even with identical eyes, they see things very differently.

Her mother helped her dress in the sweatpants and t-shirt Mr. Knight brought to the hospital, and now she is busying herself by packing up the bloody robe and nightshirt. Denise wants to tell her to leave both, but she doesn't. With her father's assistance, she stands from the gurney and takes a couple of unsteady steps.

In the emergency room, she is still surrounded by wounded police and soldiers; she sees the IVs, the bloody bandages, the nurses and doctors working frantically to save the officers. But in the midst of all the needed help, attention, and concern she finds it hard to muster up any sympathy or empathy for the injured policemen. They and their ilk killed Jeremy and shot her.

"Fuck the police," she hears herself saying.

"What?" her father asks, "What did you say?"

"Nothing, Daddy, just thinking out loud."

"Oh, ok." He takes a step with her, "I have the prescriptions for antibiotics and the pain medicine the doctor wrote. We will get them filled after you see our doctor if he agrees."

To her right is an officer on a gurney. What catches her eye is his boots. They are smeared with blood.

"How is it outside?" She asks both her parents.

"The Gaza Strip," her father answers. "And that is no exaggeration," he nods.

Her mother steps to them with book bag in tow.

"These people have lost their minds. There seems to be a fire on every block and Black people are walking the streets armed with rifles across their backs and pistols in their hands. The police are driving by armed Black people as if they don't see them, and the city buses are still running. Can you imagine seeing a group of Blacks with guns getting on a city bus? I saw that driving here. They boarded the bus with their guns out in the open."

Her mother, dressed in navy blue "because it makes me look smaller," hoists Denise's book bag up further on her shoulder.

Her father places his arm across her back for support.

"It appears that the police are only protecting the downtown area, City University, state and city buildings, and of course the mayor's neighborhood and areas like his."

"Just say it, daddy. White neighborhoods."

She is standing, but leaning heavily on her father's shoulder.

Her mother snaps the backpack straps closed, and says, "Well, it is the Blacks making all the trouble. For mercy's sake, who ever heard of shooting at the police? Those people have lost their minds, and so many of them have guns. It was very dangerous driving to this neighborhood. When you get outside, you will see. The city is being crippled by the Blacks."

Standing causes her thigh to throb with pain, but her mother's words assault her head and her heart. She is not ready to listen her mother condemning Black people for the actions of racist police and systemic racism. She has been trying to enlighten her mother on systemic racism since high school. Today, she just doesn't have the energy or the desire to inform.

"Take me to my apartment, Daddy."

"Oh, no, young lady, you are coming home with us. I am getting you out of this city," he says.

"But I'm in school. They will have classes, and you said it yourself, the police are protecting City University"

"Where you were staying with that Black boy is in a Black neighborhood, and those areas are not safe for a white girl. You are coming home with us," her mother demands.

"I have been living in that neighborhood for months, and the only problems I've had, Mother, have been your comments."

Her mother snorts through her sinuses, a sound that has unnerved Denise her whole life.

"Regardless, young lady, you are coming home."

"Your mother is right, Denise. Home is best at least until the overt danger has lessened. It's not safe to be white in this city."

"No Daddy. That's not true, it's not safe to be Black in this city. The police have been and are killing Black people. They killed Jeremy. The injustice is with the police, not the citizens that have been forced to defend themselves."

Standing is painful, but she is able to step away from her father's shoulder and stand and take steps on her own.

"I will go with you and see Dr. Jacobs because I do want a second opinion on the wounds, but I am coming back to my apartment. My life is here, and I have to see about Jeremy and Mr. Knight. And the paper needs me, now more than ever before. I live here. Falcon City is my home now, not New Port."

She looks from her mother to her father with what she feels is her most serious "my mind is made up" look.

"No, young lady. Your home is with us. With us and other white people where it is safe," her father says stepping closer to her allowing her to again lean on him for support. "You can go back to school after this madness settles down, or better yet, transfer to an out-of-state school away from the unrest."

She exhales, "And where would that be, Daddy? The whole country is struggling, not just Falcon City."

"But here, in this city, is where police are getting shot," her mother answers.

Denise decides not to argue with her parents because she does want the opinion of their family doctor, but if she has to, she will take a cab from the doctor's office to her apartment.

Riding in the back seat of her father's classic 1978 Cutlass, she sees her mother was not exaggerating. People are walking down the streets armed, and the police are not engaging them. She doesn't see one stopped Falcon City police car. They are all in motion. She does see stationary military vehicles parked on some corners with soldiers standing around them, but Falcon City police are moving.

"The military is preparing for something," Denise says.

"Enforcing the curfew would be my guess," her father answers.

"We have to get away from here. These people are crazy."

"What people, Mother?"

"Those people," she answers pointing to people walking the avenue, "those people out there with guns; they are crazy."

"Jeremy was out there, Mother. He didn't have a gun, but he was out there. I was out there, Mother. I didn't have a gun, but I was out there. Jeremy died; the police shot him down, and he didn't have a gun. I was shot and I didn't have a gun. Those people out there with guns, the police are not shooting them down, so who is really crazy, Mother?"

"Why were you out there, Denise?"

"Because, Daddy, Jeremy's best friend, Clinton" . . . the memory of Clinton standing aflame stops her, "Clinton was in trouble. Jeremy ran out to help, and I followed him. The police told him to stop, but Clinton was on fire in the middle of the street. Jeremy ran to him anyway, and they shot him."

"And you ran to Jeremy?"

"No, I stopped, but they still shot me."

"This isn't a situation the police are used to," her father says.

"Yes, you're right. They usually shoot unarmed citizens."

"That's not what I meant."

"I know, Daddy, I know."

Her head starts pounding, and it is hurting worse than her thigh and her shoulder. She leans back in the seat and closes her eyes. Jeremy is dead she thinks.

"What I'm going to do?" she asks the universe.

"About what, dear?" her mother asks.

Denise is about to answer, but the back window of her father's classic Cutlass is shattered. Glass spews all over her and the back seat. A brick tumbles over her shoulder into her lap.

"What the fuck?" she screams.

Her father slams on the brakes, causing the tires to squeal as he pulls to the side of the avenue stopping the car.

Denise is more than startled. Her whole body is trembling as she checks the surroundings expecting to see a gang approaching. Someone had to throw the brick. But she sees no one approaching their car. Her mother and father are doing the same, searching the afternoon pedestrians for an approaching crowd; there is none.

Denise looks behind the classic Cutlass and sees bricks hitting the street. She looks up and sees a burning building beginning to crumble. Flames are eating the building from the inside out.

"Oh my God," is her mother's plea, "it's going to collapse. Drive, Fredrick!"

And her father puts the classic Cutlass back into drive and hits the gas pedal, again causing the tires to squeal.

"They are destroying the city," her mother says.

Denise doesn't reply.

Chapter Ten

Dr. Talbert had received several calls from the APS President. They finally coordinated a meeting at Dr. Talbert's home, which was on City University property two blocks from the university building that held his office. Breeze pulls into the Dr. Talbert's driveway and exhales. It has been a stressful drive.

"I hear you," Melody agrees with his release.

Breeze gets out of his Camry and opens the back door for Dr. Talbert. He helps him out of the low seat into a weakened stance. He hears Dr. Talbert's hips and knees cracking.

"The old gray mare ain't what she used to be," Dr. Talbert owns.

"None of us are, sir."

Breeze continues to assist until Dr. Talbert takes his first step toward the house.

Melody walks up behind Breeze.

"He's gotten old."

"Yeah, he wasn't young when we met him."

"That is true."

They stood in the late morning sun watching him climb the four steps to his house.

"Why do you think President Nelson wants to meet with us?" she asks.

"A change in plans, new assignments, who knows?"

"I haven't gotten assignments from the President before, and I have never been involved in any planning."

"Things are different today."

"True, different and revealing."

Dr. Talbert gets the front door open, and they walk up the stairs into his house.

When they enter, his housekeeper, Agnes, who Breeze suspects is either a relative or former patient, greets them at the door in a maid's uniform. Initially, he thought she was Dr. Talbert's lover, and he hasn't eliminated that possibility from his mind. She is looking at Dr. Talbert as if she wants to embrace him. If he were alone, Breeze is certain she would have displayed her relief of his safe arrival in an embrace.

"It is all over the news. They say there is riot at the hotel. I was worried, Clarence."

She has no greeting for Melody or Breeze, only Dr. Talbert.

"Everything is fine, Agnes. I was well-protected," he says, looking to Melody and Breeze. "Can you set the study up for a meeting of four: tea, juice and those sweet biscuits you make?"

"Yes, sir," and she exits leaving them in the foyer.

"Ok, let's make it back to the study before that pompous Nelson gets here. I want to update you both on some national directives."

Sitting at the table in his study, Dr. Talbert begins, "First, rest assured that we are not reacting to this unrest. What is happening here in Falcon City, particularly with Banks and his Freedom Protestors was predicted. We even knew how many weapons they had cached, and some might say their actions were calculated. However, what was not predicted was the armed response of the colored community. We were expecting marches and protest, not firing upon the police. There is no plan for that action. So in a sense, I guess we are reacting."

His cell phone and desk phone begin to ring. He pulls the cell from his suit coat pocket, checks the number and answers it.

"Dr. Talbert, here. What . . . no . . . has his death been confirmed? Are you certain? Yes, yes of course. I suggest we meet here," he hangs up.

He looks at Melody then Breeze.

"There will be no meeting for you two today. I suggest you go to work and await further orders. President Nelson was killed. He and several APA directors were killed when SWAT sent in a robotic bomb to end the riot."

Melody sits erect in her chair.

"Wait, SWAT killed the APS President?"

Her tone is not laden with grief. Breeze thinks he hears amusement in it.

93

"So it seems, with a robot."

He hears no amusement in Dr. Talbert's words. When he looks in his face, he sees worry.

"Ok, you two go to work. You will be contacted later."

Breeze thinks he should say something - the official head of the APS is dead. He sits looking at a smirking Melody and a pensive Dr. Talbert.

"We just wait?"

"Yes, wait for orders. Damn, this is unforeseen. You two go; I need to make some calls."

Dr. Talbert doesn't look up with his dismissal. He stands goes behind his desk and drops to his chair. He picks up the phone and starts dialing.

Outside on the porch, Melody pulls a pen and pad from her purse. She is writing something. Breeze looks around the campus neighborhood. There is no unrest, and no buildings are burning in his immediate view. In the distance, he does see columns of smoke, but on campus, it appears to be just another sunny day. Three or four students have walked by them with book bags strapped to their backs, heading to class.

"I'm cooking you dinner tonight," she says stuffing a piece of paper in his hand. "This is my address. You should know what to bring for dessert."

She turns and walks away without another word. Breeze stands smiling, watching her hips sway as she walks away.

"I am attracted to that woman."

She is obviously unmoved by President Nelson's death. Breeze looks at his watch. He doesn't have a class for another forty-five minutes. He pulls his phone from his shiny new suit coat and calls Knight.

"Hey, man," he greets when he hears Knight answering.

"You haven't heard, have you?"

"I was at the hotel," Breeze assumes.

"No, what hotel? No, I'm talking about my son, Jeremy. He's dead. The police killed him this morning."

Knight didn't say white police, but Breeze thinks white police.

"What?"

All Breeze sees in his mind is the bouncy, brown, baby boy that Jeremy was.

"No, man, you must be mistaken."

"I got to go," and Knight's line clicks to silence.

Breeze is standing at the foot of Dr. Talbert's stairs unable to move with the phone to his ear.

"Not that boy, not that boy, not that baby."

His hand drops and he walks to his car. The lecture hall for his class is two blocks away. The parking lot is a half-mile away. He backs out of Dr. Talbert's driveway and parks on the street in front of the house deciding to walk to the lecture center.

His legs are stiff with anger, but he feels the walk will ease his mind and body. He wants to talk more to Knight, but he knows this isn't the time. He locks the Camry with his keypad and drops the phone back into his suit coat. He thinks about the Black kid that took his keys earlier at the hotel, he thinks about the white officers that stopped him, and the Black officer that saved their lives, and he thinks about Dr. Talbert's words.

He has been trained to think beyond race, and race is only a tool used for the manipulation for the masses.

Having walked a block, he cuts through the campus leaving the residential area. President Nelson's words enter his mind. Educated masses are a threat to the status quo; the country should educate only true Americans. He thinks of Melody. She misunderstood and thought "true Americans" meant "white Americans." He wasn't white, but he was a true American, a patriot.

But Jeremy was dead, killed by police. Another young Black man killed by police. The Desert Eagle in the small of his back is becoming heavy.

He walks through a group of white students. They are laughing and joking, relaxed, despite the city being in turmoil. There are six of them. He has enough rounds left in his clip to end their happiness. He stops paces away from them and ponders their deaths. He surveys the area. No one else is close enough to identify him. Why should they be happy when Jeremy is dead?

He draws the pistol, but his phone vibrates in his suit coat. He holsters the gun and retrieves the phone. Melody sent him a text asking if he was still trying to be a vegetarian. He thinks about how good the cheeseburger tasted yesterday and texts, "nope." He drops the phone back into his pocket.

If he kills the group, his actions would be racially motivated. He would be killing them because they were white. No, he thinks. He would be killing them because Jeremy is dead.

He draws his pistol and fires six rounds. Each lands as a headshot. He holsters the pistol, surveys the area, and is satisfied that the shots drew no attention. He turns from the bodies and continues to class.

When he enters the lecture hall, he has to enter his code to cut on the lights. The large, dark room is flooded with light. He walks behind the podium and logs onto the desk computer and brings up today's lecture. Students are arriving early as always.

Five minutes into his lecture, the disaster alarm sounds. The sequence of buzzes indicates a shooter on campus. Following protocol, Breeze has the students gather at the foot of the lecture hall in front of the podium. Some follow his directives while others flee out of the doors. The twenty or so students around him are quiet, awaiting his next directive. He logs onto computer for the update:

Shots fired on campus.

All are ordered to stay in their classrooms until the all-clear siren is sounded.

Breeze relays the information to the students as it appears on the screen.

There is a group gasp that almost causes him to laugh. What did they expect? He wonders briefly, but he knows what they expected. They expected not to be touched, to be safe despite what was happening in Falcon City. The unrest was not to spread to the City University campus. These walls are hallowed. Not anymore, Breeze thinks.

"Please take a seat in the first rows. The situation will be handled shortly," he tells them, and they comply, until shots are heard directly outside the lecture hall.

It isn't Black students that enter with guns, but white students dressed in fatigues with military vests. They fire upon the two Black students sitting together in the second row. Both students hit the floor, and the bullets riddle the lecture hall chairs. They turn their rifles to Breeze, who ducks behinds the podium. The bullets easily pass through the thin podium and strike the wall behind him. Breeze crawls the end of the display board stands and fires. He drops both assailants, but his clip is empty. Students bolt from the lecture hall.

Breeze walks to the corpses at the top of the lecture center. He recognizes both as students in his class. One would have probably gotten a 'B' out of the class. The other one was failing. On thc 'B' student's hip, Breeze spots a Desert Eagle 9mm. He removes the gun from the holster and ejects the clip. He pats the corpse down and finds two other clips. Both corpses are armed with modified AR-15s.

When he walks out of the lecture center onto the yard of the campus, he is immediately fired upon. He drops to the concrete sidewalk and locates the threat in a marksman stance with an AR-15 sighted on him. Breeze rolls, avoiding the rapid shots, until he gets to a metal garbage can, which he topples for cover. The marksman continues to fire.

"Die, you nigger motherfucker!" The student yells as he fires.

From behind him Breeze hears rounds firing. He turns to see one of the Black students from the lecture hall armed with an assailant's AR-15. He drops the marksman after several rounds. The other student also emerges with an assailant's rifle as well. They run past Breeze into the yard, firing at the military-clad students. They don't make it very far. Breeze sees both fall, but from behind the garbage can he is able to pick off three more shooters. Breeze sees one lone shooter remaining. He is searching for a target. He spots an Asian student crouched behind a tree. He fires rapid rounds until the tree finally topples. Breeze stands and fire two shots, each yielding pink mist from the bullets exiting the target's skull.

Black, Spanish, Asian and Arab students and faculty are scattered dead across the yard of the campus. Breeze counts five shooters, seven when he includes the two that came into the lecture hall. What he should do is stay in the yard because he hears the approaching sirens in the distance. What he does is walk to Melody's building with his pistol in his hand.

People are rapidly exiting the building. Only he is entering. When he gets into the stairwell, he sees Melody with a group descending the stairs. He exhales and holsters his pistol.

"I'm leaving," she says when she gets to bottom of the stairs.

"I agree, let's get to my car."

People are leaving the campus on foot, in cars, and on bikes. Falcon City police and the military are entering from all arteries. When they arrive at the car, Dr. Talbert is standing on his porch.

"Come on in," he directs.

Breeze sees Melody hesitating, "It's safer inside . . . less chance of being stopped by police or shot by deranged students." He doesn't fear either, but he wants her to stay close, close enough to protect.

She shakes her head no.

"I doubt that there is a safe place in this city," but she walks up the walkway to the stairs and takes them two at a time.

In the study, they return to their seats at the table, and Dr. Talbert sits behind his desk. The table is covered with a rust-colored leather pad that has a thick black felt bottom. Breeze is looking at how exact it matches the top of the table, and he suspects the two, the table and padded top, were manufactured together. The chairs and the table were probably crafted for a small dining room during an era when families ate at the dining room table. The table, pad, and chairs are all antiques, Breeze guesses from the forties.

"Lord, what a mess. What do you know?" Dr. Talbert asks them.

Melody answers first, "Armed white students opened fire on non-whites. True Americans have lost their fucking minds."

She sits back in the chair.

Dr. Talbert looks at him; Breeze tilts his head, and raises his eyebrows. Melody's words surprised him. He decides to tone the report down a little.

"Kids in fatigues and AR-15s were indiscriminately firing on students and faculty."

"White kids," Melody interjects, "and they were targeting non-whites in the yard during lunch. They executed a plan picking the most populated time. I doubt that it was in response to riots in Falcon City. Those hatful little bastards had this in their minds for a while."

She looks at both men with challenge in her eyes as if she expected a rebuttal argument.

"How many shooters?" Dr. Talbert asks.

"Seven in the yard area," Breeze answers.

"Did the shooting occur anywhere else on campus?"

"Not from the early security police reports. The warning stated shots fired in the yard."

Melody sits erect in the chair.

"No one expected this."

Breeze expected the alarms to sound due to the students he shot, but she is right, he didn't expect armed students with AR-15s.

"It could have been worse had the police not been on campus," Dr. Talbert states.

Breeze clears his throat.

"It wasn't the police that killed them; it was myself and a couple of students."

He places his open palm on the leather pad and rubs his fingertips into the grain. Unsanctioned kills have been a problem for him in the past. He was disciplined for two: he beat a man to death who he found raping a girl in a park, and he stabbed a man to death who tried to rob him when he was first released from the state hospital.

"What? You and students?"

Dr. Talbert looks like he is about to stand but thinks better of it. He moves a file on his desk as if it was blocking his line of vision. He looks directly at Breeze and says, "Tell me that again."

Breeze has folded under his fingers leaving his knuckles and thumbs to slide across the grain of the leather pad.

"Yes, sir. Two armed students entered my lecture and opened fire. I returned fire, killing the two. Outside on the yard, I was fired upon again. Two Black students secured the rifles of the two assailants that entered the lecture hall and engaged the shooters. They were both killed, but they assisted in stopping the threat."

With his eyes still on Breeze, Dr. Talbert acknowledges, "You have had a violent morning, Noble."

Breeze nods his head in the affirmative, but he doesn't mention the six students he killed before the attack, or the death of Jeremy.

Turning to Melody, Dr. Talbert continues with, "And you as well, how are you holding up?"

Sitting on the edge of her chair she admits, "Sir, actually, I am feeling very threatened."

Breeze stops moving his thumbs and listens closer.

"That is understandable, with the intentions of the attack," Dr. Talbert responds.

Melody lowers her head and swings it from left to right repeatedly. She looks at Dr. Talbert and says, "No, honestly sir, I began feeling threatened at the APS meeting this morning. The incident here on campus only confirmed what I felt."

Her words don't state anger, but Breeze hears it in her tone. She sounds angry and fed up.

"Tell me more," is the query from Dr. Talbert.

"Well, sir, the times we are living in scare me. When I was sick, I didn't have this . . . fear . . . this anger. I know that historically, Blacks in this country have been treated less than whites from slavery to now. We have always been thought of as less, but during my sickness, it was only a thought. Now, sir, thinking better . . . the injustice scares me. The police killing Blacks at will with little to no consequence is frightening in itself, but hearing President Nelson speaking of the advantages and the actions the APS has taken and will take to the benefit of true Americans threatened me personally."

"Why?" Dr. Talbert asks.

Melody places her hands on the table's pad and sighs.

"Because sir, I am not white, and I interpreted "true Americans" to mean "white Americans.""

Her words don't falter.

"Ah, see that is where you error. The American Purist Society is not concerned with race. A person of any ethnicity can be a true American. Being white doesn't make me a true American, what makes me a true American is loving this country. What makes me a true American is being loyal to this country despite its flaws. Those students who took arms today aren't true Americans. Their actions endangered the safety of this nation. They are no different than Banks and his Freedom Protestors. They are loyal only to their whiteness. They and others like them feel superior due to the color of their skin. That is not an American belief; that is the belief of a racist. And we, the American Purist society, view racists as traitors because their loyalty is to their skin, not to their country."

Breeze is familiar with the expression on Dr. Talbert's face, and he is certain Melody is too. This is how he looks when he is teaching: direct eye contact, leaning forward listening, and alert eyes checking to make sure his message is hitting home.

Breeze notices that Melody does not have the expression of a receptive student; in fact, she appears hostile. Breeze is familiar with the expression on her face as well.

Putting her hands on nylon-covered knees and leaning forward in the chair, she asks, "Ok, sir. Answer this for me: why were all the schools that Nelson spoke of closing in neighborhoods of color?"

Dr. Talbert offers a half-smile.

"It is to garner support for school closings in general. The public has to get used to the idea of school closings, so we start with easy ones first. Due to the racist attitude of the city, those schools, the ones in neighborhoods of color, are low-hanging fruit if you will.

"Don't get me wrong, we know racism exists, and we use it to our advantage, but using it doesn't make us racist. Eventually, the school closings will happen in white neighborhoods as well, but you are right. We start in the neighborhoods of color because there is less protest from those areas."

Melody is shaking her head no.

"So, what you are telling me is that my people are being targeted, but it's ok because white schools will be targeted later?"

Dr. Talbert nods, "In short, yes."

"So, white schools aren't the target now, and apparently neither are white people because I can count on one hand the number of unarmed white people the police killed last year . . ."

She looks to Breeze for the first time since sitting down at the table then she looks back at Dr. Talbert.

"As a Black person living in these times, in this country, the last thing I want to see is more and better armed police which is it what President Nelson and the APS want. How can I not feel threatened? How can any Black person living in this country not feel threatened? The APS may not be racist, but the police are, and the APS wants more police."

There is always an irritating scent present in Dr. Talbert's home, and while listening intently to Melody, Breeze's mind finally deciphers what the smell is. The odor is made up of two things: green rubbing alcohol and mothballs. In a quick intellectual snap, a years-old the mystery was solved, and he credits the insight to Melody.

She thinks differently than he, and listening to her brings new thoughts in his mind. He opens his fingers again on the leather grain of the pad, and with palms down. He returns his full attention to the conversation.

"No, not really," Dr. Talbert informs shaking his head to the negative. "It is not about merely arming police. We are diverting funds from education, and to divert those funds we need a reason, and American fear is lessened with a police presence. True, some Americans are racist and their agendas can support ours for the time being. The truth is white racists don't have a problem funding police."

Melody raises her hand in traffic cop fashion and extends her index finger, she doesn't point at Dr. Talbert, Breeze notices, but her finger is pointing to the ceiling.

"But there is no denying that police are killing Black people, Dr. Talbert."

He responds with equal urgency.

"Yes, but we must keep the end game in mind, Melody. The problem is an educated mass. When the majority of the country is educated, the status quo is at risk."

"But the status quo should be at risk."

She is close to shouting, with both hands raised to her ears and fingers spread wide.

"Society can't grow and advance with old thinking. Old thoughts should be moved out for new ideas. You taught me that. My old thinking was sick, so I had to change. This country's thinking is sick. It wants things to stay as it always was: white supremacy, fossil fuels, rich getting richer, homophobia are all thoughts of the past, and keeping those thoughts, maintaining the status quo, will retard the growth of this nation. Society is a living and breathing creature. It is supposed to change and adapt. Fighting against change is a denial of realty, something else you taught me, sir.

"The students that were shooting on campus were living in denial. They couldn't accept people of color on the campus. What are people like that going to do when people of color are the majority? How are they going to accept Asian police, Spanish teachers, and Arab preachers? The old status quo has no acceptance of such changes.

"When you say the APS views the education of the masses as a threat to the status quo, you are telling me and my people to sit on the back of the bus and shut the fuck up. You are telling gay couples to stay hidden in the closet, and you are telling women to stay barefoot and pregnant."

She exhales a long breath, her shoulders slump, and she sits back in the chair.

"I guess what I am saying, Dr. Talbert, is fuck the status quo, and fuck the APS."

Dr. Talbert doesn't answer her. Breeze sees him look to the doorway and signal with his hand to lower something. Breeze looks to the doorway and sees Agnes with a Colt .45 pointed at him and a Smith and Wesson .357 pointed at Melody. He wonders whether she could handle the recoil from both weapons if she fired them, but the stealthy way she entered the doorway and the death-cold gaze of her gray eyes tells him she could.

She lowers the weapons, but remains in the doorway.

"Melody, I am going to consider the stress of the day and ignore the resignation you just gave me. I expect you in the office tomorrow morning at eight."

He looks to Breeze.

"I trust the information you both gave me about the shooters is correct. So we can assume the school will be open to administration since the threat has been eliminated. Noble, I will make some calls and have your involvement in the shooting removed. You both made the right decision leaving campus. I have another meeting scheduled, so good afternoon."

He dismisses them both, again.

"No rebuttal?" Melody asks.

"There is no point. I am convinced you believe your argument is valid."

Breeze is dumbstruck by Melody's noncompliance with APS thought, her fearless verbiage against what Dr. Talbert has taught them, and by her honest admission of fear.

He is not afraid of America, but he understands why Melody would be. She is more Afro-American than American. Like Knight, her loyalties are racial. So she feels threatened by this society and it's status quo. As a patriot, he is part of society, but he understands her doubt. What she doesn't understand is that she is part of the status quo. As APS agents, they both are part of the American system. He will help her to see the part she plays. The thought of helping her causes him to grin.

"Sir," Melody says to Dr. Talbert, "I don't want you to not consider my resignation from the APS. I will report to work tomorrow as your secretary, but I cannot and will not accept any more APS assignments."

Breeze feels his chest tightening. His first assignment was to eliminate an APS agent who wanted to resign. Melody had to know that walking away wasn't an option for an agent.

"We will discuss this tomorrow in private," is Dr. Talbert's answer.

Chapter Eleven

Denise's family doctor added sutures and exchanged the gauze bandage for a clear adhesive bandage to cover her gunshot wounds. He had told her and her parents the prescriptions were fine, but she should be on bed rest for at least seventy-two hours.

Driving to her parents' home, she hears the report on the City University shootings.

"No, is that true?" she asks.

"Did they say white shooters?" her mother asks.

"Six professors, and twenty-three students dead. No way are you going back to that campus or your apartment," her father declares.

Sitting between her father and mother in the front seat, with the wind blowing through the car from the shattered back window, with her shoulder and thigh throbbing from the gunshot wounds, and thinking of Jeremy being dragged to the curb like garbage, she resigns in her mind to going to her parents' home, too much is happening too fast. She can't wrap her mind around the situation.

"Did they say white shooters?" her mother asks again. "Why would white people be shooting on campus?"

Denise tells her, "There was a white supremacy group that met on campus, Mother. They were a registered student group that claimed the Rebel flag spoke to their culture. They were granted access to student services due to being classified under cultural studies.

"They seemed harmless from afar. I never went to any of their meetings, but others did. They always served free beer and pizza, so a lot of kids went. They weren't the Klan or anything, just a group that was proud of their Southern heritage. I never thought of them as a real danger."

And she hadn't. They were just another student group.

"But you think they could have done the shooting?" Her father asks.

"They would be my first guess."

Her mother reaches for and holds onto Denise's hand. "How could the school allow such a group?"

"Cultural studies: there are Asian groups, and Mexican group - almost all ethnicities have student organizations. There are Irish and Polish groups too. The administration and student government try to be inclusive."

"My goodness, it seems like someone should be in charge to oversee the meetings or something."

Denise doesn't comment because she remembers when Jeremy tried to start a student Panthers group. The opposition he faced from both the administration and the student government was formidable. He was denied a charter due to the political past associated with the name Panthers. When she thinks about it, the only Black organization on campus is the Jazz Club, and its membership is fifty percent white.

Once they get to New Port, her father pulls into the driveway of their four-car garage and opens the overhead door. She sees his Lexus truck, used for pulling the boat, her mother's Saab, and the BMW her dad drives daily. He parks the classic Cutlass in the empty spot on the end.

"You are going to have to use the upstairs guest room until we can have Angela air out and change the linen in your room. She comes in the morning, so it will only be tonight," her mother says, holding the car door open for her.

Her father comes around and helps her stand.

"You seem to be in pain, Princess."

"I am, Daddy."

He hadn't called her Princess in years. The endearment makes her smile despite the throbbing. She leans heavily on him walking into the house. He helps her up both flights of stairs and down the hallway to the guest bedroom.

She doesn't hesitate to grab the remote and cut on the television.

"Well, I'm going to leave you to it. I need to lie down myself. That drive got to me."

"I'm sure, Daddy."

After her father leaves, she sits at the bottom of the bed and finds a news channel. The brunette reporter with green eyes is standing in front of the campus chapel near tears. She's saddened by what she's seen.

"The carnage is unbelievable. Never in the school's history has such an act of violence occurred. The police are slow to label the shooting a hate crime, but when one sees the attire of the suspected shooters and the twenty-nine victims of color and the six white heroes who sacrificed their lives trying to stop the shooters before they could reach the yard, the nature of the shooting becomes painfully clear. The shooting drew both military and Falcon City police. Both are being overextended as our city erupts in unprecedented violence."

With her finger on her earpiece, the reporter says, "I am being told that the military and Falcon City police have just stopped a caravan of ten vans and trucks filled with armed men at the city limits. We are going to a live feed now."

Denise instantly sees the reporter's estimation was wrong. She counts over thirty vans and trucks plowing through the military and police line. The trucks are not being stopped.

"Oh, my God," her mother says entering the guestroom, "they are running over police and soldiers."

Denise is momentarily speechless, but sadly she is not surprised.

"They are probably late. I'll bet they were supposed to be there at the University with those kids. This was to be their backup."

"No, don't say that. You are being paranoid. People don't plan such things. You are not thinking right after being shot."

"I was shot and kicked in the head by people who think just like these morons driving trucks though the police and the army. Oh, my God, look at them. They're not stopping."

The helicopter camera follows the caravan, and as Denise predicted, they drive into the neighborhood of City University. The school is surrounded by a poor Black neighborhood. The police and military are shown preventing them from entering the actual campus. The camera follows vans and trucks driving through the poor neighborhood. They are shooting at pedestrians from the trucks and vans. There is no reporter feed, no audio, only the image of people firing from the vehicles at members of the community. The University area is secure, but the surrounding neighborhood becomes a war zone.

People are seen coming from their houses and apartments firing back at the trucks and vans and throwing Molotov cocktails. Denise thinks of the building they saw crumbling from fire earlier. Neighborhood structures like that building are barely standing.

"The neighborhood will burn to the ground," she says, watching the fighting.

"Maybe it should," are her mother's weary words.

When a truck or van stops, it is set aflame by a Molotov cocktail. When a person exits a truck they are shot or chased back into a truck by gunfire. The neighborhood is not surrendering easily.

"Where did they get so many guns?"

"Who, Mother, the attackers or the residents of the neighborhood?"

"Well, both really. I know white people have guns, but I didn't know so many Black people have guns. Why aren't the police and army helping those neighborhood people? It's obvious they are being attacked."

The helicopter housing the camera vibrates form the shock of a passing jet, and then another and another.

"Ah, here comes the help," her mother says.

What they witness doesn't qualify as help to Denise. The jets are firing what Denise thinks must be massive bullets because the rounds are causing the vans and

117

trucks and parked cars to explode. The moving vehicles are shot to immobility, then they explode.

People, both the attackers and the residents, are being split into pieces by the rounds. Denise sees arms and other human body parts flying through the air. Her shoulder throbs.

Buildings are collapsing and people are running through the streets, white trails are seen and then the explosions increase in size. Whole sections of city blocks are covered with smoke. When the smoke clears only flames and craters are seen, no more homes.

The vans, the trucks, parked cars, the attackers, and the residents are gone. Only fire, smoke, craters, and City University remain.

"What happened?"

Denise's mouth is hanging open.

"What happened? Is this real? Did they really drop bombs in the city?"

Her mother drops on the bed next to her.

"Can they do that, kill Americans like that?"

"They have done it before."

"When? When has this country dropped bombs on its own people?"

"In 1921, Mother, in Tulsa, Oklahoma, and in 1985 in Philadelphia, Pennsylvania. "

"No, you are mistaken. Americans don't kill other Americans, not here in this country."

"You, we . . . just saw it happen, Mother. We just watched our country murder Americans on live television."

Chapter Twelve

They both see Dr. Talbert's house on the screen; they see white smoke, followed by flames and more smoke, and then . . . they see the crater. The house is gone.

"No."

Breeze leans forward on Melody's couch. He immediately pulls his phone from his jacket and dials Dr. Talbert's number. It gives out a busy signal. He redials and gets the same signal.

"I can't reach him. No."

He dials the number again, and again the busy signal.

"Maybe the phone lines are down," Melody's says.

"That was his house, right?"

"I think so."

"That was his house."

"What will we do if he's gone?" Melody asks.

Breeze looks to her. She is still watching the scene and talking. He understands her question. Dr. Talbert is their contact to the APS; their work assignments come through him. The only direct link they have to the American Purist Society is Dr. Talbert.

"He's not gone, maybe that wasn't his house."

"It was his house, we both know it was his house, and the limo parked in front meant that other APS

leaders were there too. You think . . .?" Her question
lingers.

"I think what?"

"Well, the police killed President Nelson this
morning."

"An accident. They were trying to quash a riot."

"Nonetheless he is dead, and now Dr. Talbert's
home with APS leaders inside is blown from existence."

"Again, coincidence. They were putting down the
unrest on the campus."

Her apartment is as sparsely furnished as his. In
her living area there is only a couch and television on
a stand, not even a coffee table to put the remote on.
So he is sitting with both the remote and phone in his
hands. Beams from the late afternoon sun illuminate
her buffed hardwood floors. His condominium floors
are carpeted.

"I think we should be very cautious. Who's to say
that the attack will stop with the leaders?"

She turns her head from the television to Breeze.

"What attack?"

"The obvious attack on the APS."

"Are you serious?"

"Open your eyes, Noble. In one morning the
leadership of the APS has been eliminated. The head is
gone. All that is left is the body."

Breeze sits back on the couch with both hands full.

"You are speaking as if Dr. Talbert being dead is a certainty. He might have left the house."

"With APS leaders in his home?"

"You are making an assumption through coincidence."

"Coincidence my ass, Noble. Look at the facts."

"But who?"

"The government, that's who. The APS is acting as a sanctioned government agency, which they are not. All their talk of subversives - shit, they, we are they subversives. A think-tank turned militia. We and the other agents are their military arm."

No, she's being paranoid, Breeze thinks.

"If what you are saying is true, we could be targeted as well."

"I think we should be very aware."

Breeze tries Dr. Talbert's number again, and again the busy signal sounds. He looks to the television screen and sees the helicopter is flying over the undamaged campus buildings. The screen blinks and returns to the reporter standing in front of the chapel, the one who called the six students he shot heroes.

"Oh, my God," is all the reporter says, and the screen blinks to blue.

Breeze turns from channel to channel. They are all off the air.

"I don't think they planned on the public seeing the attack. That helicopter was a fluke. The pilot got under the radar somehow. No way was America to see that."

Melody stands and sits right back down and looks him directly in the eye.

"Think, Noble. A think-tank with agents, a think-tank affecting government policy and legislation, a think-tank affecting the consciousness of the nation with a political agenda . . . that is the APS."

She leans back on the couch and sighs.

"Maybe they will think cutting off the head will be enough. Maybe we are not in danger."

"So you are throwing coincidence out the window?"

"Yes, I am, and so should you."

She leans forward, her brown eyes on him.

"You were killing police officers, Noble, police officers in America, to further the APS agenda."

"What?" he sits up and almost stands, but thinking of Dr. Talbert's death has him stiff. "How do you . . ."

"I knew of all your assignments. I sent most of Dr. Talbert's coded responses to Nelson. But think about what I am saying. A think-tank in America is killing American police officers. No government will allow that, not even this greedy, capitalistic one. The APS obviously went too far."

Breeze rubs his hands over his shaved head frustrated by the possibility of truth in her statements.

"You are making a huge assumption."

She smiles and grabs his hand.

"No, not really. What I am doing is connecting loose ends. Consider this: a race riot broke out in Falcon City after an APS initiative. In other words, after you completed your assignment, the city erupted."

He pulls his hand from hers.

"What?"

"No, I'm not saying it was your fault."

She holds his hand again.

"You were only following orders, but think about how the government would interpret the action, especially if they confirmed that APS was killing police, which led to the riots."

Breeze likes her touching him; the feel of his hand in hers is soothing. Her words disrupt the order of his thoughts, but her touch pulls the unrest from him. He places his other hand on top of hers.

"The police were killing Black people first. My killing the cops didn't lead to the riots."

"Oh, yes it did. You and I know that after Renaldo Banks and his group opened fire on police. Others in the city followed suit. You were framing Banks for the police killings. Banks had to know the police weren't coming to arrest him or his followers, so they opened fire. If those Falcon City police officers weren't killed, there would have been no framing of Banks and no riots.

"Blacks have been getting shot by police for decades, but the APS moved the Black community to the next level by having you kill police officers in Falcon City after the police killed a Black person elsewhere in the country. Black people within the community assumed other Blacks were already killing white cops. Your killings started this revolt; the APA started this revolt.

"The APS created a movement a pseudo revolution by having you kill those officers. They started these riots, and the government ended them and the APS with the military strike. Don't you see it?"

What she is saying is plausible to Breeze.

"Why now?"

"The opportunity presented itself. No one was expecting the Black community to offer an armed response or white supremacists to be trucked in. It was an extreme situation and the government took full advantage of it. The APS is dead."

Again, she has disrupted his mind.

"But the APS made me. We are APS agents. My life revolves around the Society. My directives come from them. They made me."

"No, Noble."

She squeezes his hand.

"You made you with Dr. Talbert's guidance, just like I made me with his guidance. He is dead, the APS is dead, but I am still here. My life is still here. I am going to work tomorrow like any other secretary. I will be shocked by my boss' death and wait for reassignment like any other civil servant in the union. I work for the State, and I have eleven years seniority. They will place me with another professor or in another department or at another school. My life will go on. I am the woman Dr. Talbert helped me to become. This cover is me, and it's solid. Just because the APS is dead doesn't mean I am dead."

Her words don't make any sense to him.

"Life will go on. The APS is dead."

He pulls his hands from hers and stands, but doesn't take a step.

"He was my father."

She looks up at him.

"No, he was a psychologist who used us to further the APS agenda. We were his tools, not his children. He was a man who helped us for his own gain. He took us broken, and put us back together with APS goals in mind. He made us whole, but whole APS assassins. I will survive without him, and so will you."

He forces himself to sit.

"No, I don't think I will."

"You will because you have. You have been surviving on your own all this time. He only guided us."

Breeze looks down into Melody's hopeful face and knows the situation is not as simple as she makes it sound. He has been able to live his life as he lived it by following APS directives. He followed orders and did what he was told. He believed in what the APS stood for, and he believed what Dr. Talbert told him was the truth. How could he not?

Before Dr. Talbert, Breeze existed by responding to life. If he was hungry he ate, when he was thirsty he drank, and what he needed he took. He was in and out of jail, homeless, and trapped in delusional thinking before Dr. Talbert.

Dr. Talbert and the APS showed him how to fit into society without white skin. They showed him how to be a true American, and they taught him that it wasn't about race. When he was sick, he believed he needed to be white to fit into society, and he took the skin he needed. Through Dr. Talbert and the APS, he learned he didn't need white skin to be a true American.

Being a true American was about being loyal and dedicated to America, and he was. It wasn't about skin color. Dr. Talbert had explained that to him a hundred times if he explained it once. Dr. Talbert was loyal to America, not his white skin, and he trained Breeze to

127

be loyal to America and not his brown skin. Melody and Knight had it wrong because they wanted to be loyal to their skin and not to their country.

They were no different than the deranged students at City University, or the cops that killed Jeremy, or the white racists who attacked Falcon City. Breeze knew better. He was loyal and dedicated to his country.

But if Melody is right, his country killed Dr. Talbert and the APS, his guides to his current and better life. If both the APS and Dr. Talbert are gone, so is he, Dr. Noble Breeze. How can he exist without those who made him? He sits looking at the snow on the television screen.

Who is to be his guide, who will remind him that it's not about race, who will tell him that he is trained to think above race despite what he sees and feels, who will keep him thinking like an APS agent rather than an angry Afro-American? Who will stop him from defocusing?

"They made me," he says barely audible.

Melody pushes his shoulder and says, "No, Noble, you made you. They pointed out the path but you cleared the brush, you did the studying, you passed the classes, you completed APS training, you changed your thinking, you changed your behavior. Yes, Dr.

Talbert helped us both, but he didn't make us. We made us. Understand?"

How can she be so wrong? How can she understand so little? Breeze quickly leans over to her. He is less than inch from her face.

"We didn't make "us." "Us" was running around the state hospital crazy as hell, "us" skinned a white boy. "Us" ate a patient's eye. "Us" was born in an alley garbage can. They made us who we are now, and if they are gone, so are we. Do you understand?"

He would be helping her by putting a bullet in her confused head. She is confused and paranoid, and spreading both to him. If she were dead, order would be restored to his mind. He would be able to think. Her words are confusing his thought. He doesn't move his eyes from her face, and neither does she.

"You don't scare me, Noble, because I know when you are trying to be scary, and I know when you are scared."

He moves back a bit from her face.

"You are scared now because the principal person in your life is gone; but this life is change. That is how we know we are alive, because things change and we survive."

He leans away from her and rests back on the couch.

"One thing is certain. Dr. Talbert and the APS prepared us for change by letting us know we could change. Shit, Noble, we changed from institution patients to productive members of society. What Dr. Talbert did do for us was let us know we can change. If he and the APS made us, so what? We don't have to stay what they created, and we can survive without them that's all I'm saying."

Now she is leaning to him, an inch away from his face.

"Do you hear me, Noble?"

She smiles and kisses his lips.

He closes his eyes and allows the kiss to drain confusion and anger from his mind. Her touch soothes him. She kisses him again.

"We are survivors. You and I are still here."

He opens his eyes and he feels the smile on his face, and he initiates a third kiss. Her lips taste like butterscotch.

"I have to go see a friend. Do you mind riding with me?" He asks.

He quickly kisses her again then stands from the couch and drops the remote on the cushion.

"No, I don't mind at all. I want to see outside for myself."

Chapter Thirteen

Her mother brings dinner up to her in the guestroom. Denise sits alone on the bed with the plate on her lap. Her father is enforcing the doctor's bed-rest order and won't let her come down to dinner.

The last time she ate steak she was at her parents' home. In the neighborhood she lived in with Jeremy, good steaks were seldom seen in the stores, and when they were seen they were priced out of their student budget, and it was the same with fresh vegetables. The only time she ate fresh produce was on campus. She is enjoying the steak, the peas, and the carrots.

The news is repeating, so she picks up the remote and cuts off the television. They used their laptops for television, she and Jeremy. The remote drops to the bed. She sighs and picks back up her knife and fork and slices into the steak and thinks of calling Mr. Knight, but the thought distresses her, and causes her shoulder and thigh to throb.

In the bed, with the television off, away from her mother's ignorant questions, and with the plate of good food and the peaceful floral décor of the room around her, she is able to exhale. There was no exhaling in Falcon City, and not even in the hospital. She feels as if she has been holding her breath since Jeremy ran out of their apartment onto the street. Now she exhales. Now she is able to think.

Everything she loved is either gone or changed. She forks up a fork full of green peas to her mouth. They are tender and sweet. Very little in Falcon City will be tender and sweet anymore. Their love was tender and sweet. Jeremy was the gentlest lover she had ever had. He loved her, but Falcon City changed him, too. No, not Falcon City, the police shootings changed Jeremy. The police killing Black people changed him. She slices another piece from the steak and chews it with satisfaction.

It wasn't about her being white or him being Black when they started dating. It was about love. They couldn't stop looking at each other from the moment they met. Neither his father nor her parents were happy when they moved in together, but they didn't care. It was the two of them against the world . . . but the world won. She puts the fork down in the plate.

Eventually, the world made them realize that she was white and he was Black. The police, waitresses, people in the neighborhood, the University, and even working at The Blackman's Journal reminded them that they were from two separate worlds. But when they made love, there was the oneness that held them together regardless of the world's interference. They loved each other. But now he is gone, taken by the world.

She tries the peas, but they are no longer sweet to her palate. She puts the fork down, again. Why return to a place no longer sweet? When she thinks of the apartment, she thinks of the police dragging Jeremy to the curb, she thinks of Clinton burning alive, and she thinks of Jeremy not stopping.

She looks over at the phone on the night table. She knows the number. She has always been good at remembering numbers. She picks up the receiver and enters Mr. Knight's home number on the dial pad.

"Hello?"

"Good evening, Mr. Knight."

"Denise?"

"Yes, sir, it's me."

"I was just praying for you, girl. I called up to the hospital and they told me you were discharged. Are you with your parents? You didn't go back to the apartment, did you?"

"Yes, sir, I am with my folks. I don't know if I will ever go back to the apartment."

"I understand. The building is mine, and I will get your stuff to you, so don't worry."

"I know, and I'm not worried about my stuff. How are you, Mr. Knight?"

"Tired, baby. Real tired."

"I understand."

"I met with the mayor, and he assured us that there will be an investigation into the shooting."

"I don't care, Mr. Knight. None of that: the investigation, the riots, or the burning of the city will bring Jeremy back."

"It won't, baby, it won't."

"I'm not coming back, Mr. Knight, to the Journal, Falcon City, or the University. It's all just too much."

"No, baby, don't make those type of decisions right now. Give yourself time to breathe and grieve. Don't let pain think for you. You are a smart girl with a bright future. Give yourself time to think. I would hate to see you turn your back on your plans. You are too smart of a girl to give up. Jeremy wouldn't want that. Understand?"

She hears him, but says, "It's just too much, sir."

"For now, it's too much, but time heals us. Trust me. I will have Mildred call you when we get all funeral arrangements finalized, ok?"

"Yes of course. Good night, Mr. Knight."

"Good night, baby. I will keep praying for you."

Denise puts the receiver back in the cradle. She feels the tears creeping down her cheeks. She will go back to Falcon City to bury Jeremy, but nothing else.

"People are evil and crazy and filled with hate," she says to the darkened television screen.

"But they get better, Princess."

Her father walks into the room.

"No, they don't, Daddy. The study of history has taught me that. People are evil. This country was built on the annihilation of a people, and on the enslavement of another people, and not just American society, but all of Western society - no, all of civilization was built on brutality: wars, domination, genocide, and injustice are the way of man. People are evil, Daddy, and they always have been."

She doesn't have to say another word to her father. She's certain her words are true, and there is no point in arguing the facts. But, she knows her father, and he loves America, so she expects him to have a rebuttal, one she doesn't want to hear.

"No, Princess, we do what we have to, to survive. People war for resources like any other animal, but what separates us from animals is the societies we build from our brutality. Sacrifices are made for the betterment of mankind. There would be no America if Europeans hadn't invaded the land, and the country couldn't have been built without free labor. Yes, many were sacrificed, but the establishment of this country was worth it. Never in the history of man has a country done as much good as America."

Against every fiber in her body, she asks, "What good, Daddy? Tell me, because all I see is domination for profit. All I see is a nation of merchants with wealth and a powerful army driven by greed. What good do we do for the sake of good? What good do we do that isn't linked to profit?"

He father looks down at her shaking his head.

"No, you are not seeing things clearly. We feed the world, Princess. We send medicine to poor countries. We spread democracy across the globe. We remove evil dictators and bring human rights to those who need it. We keep peace in the world. If it wasn't for America, evil would rule."

"And tell me, Daddy; what is evil?"

"Evil is dictators starving their people while filling their own pockets, evil is refusing to let women have a fair chance, evil is committing genocide, evil is having children strap on bombs, evil is keeping people in the dark ages by not educating them, evil is raping young girls. Evil is not giving people a say in their own lives, and forcing leaders upon them. America fights against all of these things, Princess. Our country has done some wrongs, but we have done a lot of good."

His words, his beliefs confirm that she can't stay with her parents. Their truths would force her into a regression that would cripple her for life. She has been educated beyond their beliefs.

"Ok, Daddy. America is good."

She says deciding against arguing. His beliefs are his.

"I'm getting sleepy now. Do you mind if I turn in?"

She is tired, but also, she doesn't want to hear her father sing the praises of the country that killed Jeremy.

"You are patronizing me, but I understand. I thought my parents were old fogies who didn't see reality, too. I was just checking on you, Princess. And your mother sent me up for the dishes and to see if you wanted any homemade custard."

She hands him her plate from her lap.

"Yes Daddy, that sounds really nice. I would love some custard, and I wasn't patronizing you. I am just agreeing to disagree because I am tired."

He takes her plate and says, "I will be right back."

I have to get out of here, she thinks again, "but go where." The apartment is out. No way can she go back there. Too much of Jeremy is there.

"You are running from the fight. You know where the battle is," she hears herself saying.

She stands and her thigh aches.

"I have battle scars."

Her shoulder begins to hurt, too. She carefully sits back down on the bed.

"I'm not running from the fight because it's not really my battle. It was mine when I was with Jeremy, but Jeremy is dead. Jeremy."

She begins to weep.

~~~~~~

"You should have stopped. You saw the guns. You heard the shots. Why did you even go out there? You saw them shooting, but you ran out there anyway. You ran out there and they shot you. You could have stayed inside were it was safe. It was safe inside with me, with me."

She stands.

"Enough, tears won't change a thing."

But she can't stop them.

Her mother enters the room with box of tissues and a full bowl of custard and a spoon. All she wants is the custard, not the conversation she is certain her mother will start.

"You know, it occurred to me last week while I was making this batch that I haven't passed this recipe on to you. I got it from my mother, she got from hers, and my grandmother got her from her mother. So while you are here, we are going to make a batch." She puts the box of tissues in Denise's hands. "Sit."

She slowly lowers to the bed, and her mother sits next to her. She pulls tissues from the box and wipes her tears.

"It wasn't that I didn't like the boy, it's just that I didn't want my grandchildren to be Black in this country. Black people have it harder here. I know that, and I didn't want any of mine to be burdened with all of that prejudice and stuff. All it takes is a drop of

Black blood and people will treat them like second-class citizens. But I liked the boy, and he was good for you. Your grades got better once you moved in with him. I'm not prejudiced, despite what you think. I'm just practical."

She hands Denise the bowl of custard.

Practical, Denise thinks. How is realizing that injustice exist but accepting it practical? What is practical about knowing that Black Americans are treated like second-class citizens, but that treatment is ok as long as none of her lineage is Black? She didn't want Black grandbabies, but Jeremy was good for Denise - good enough to improve her grades, but not good enough to procreate with.

Denise looks at the custard and says, "Yes, I suppose being Black is a burden in this country, one I am sure Black people are aware of, and you are right, Black people are treated like second-class citizens, but who is treating them like that? Is it white people, is it the laws of this country, is it corporate America, is it the police, is it the courts, is it Black people accepting the second-class citizen status?

"Jeremy refused to accept being a second-class citizen, Mother. I see that now. He had the right to protect, to be concerned, and to care about his friend. As an American, he had the right to run out there and check on the wellbeing of his friend. He was refusing his second-class citizen standing when he ran out there on that street. And when the police shot him down, they were enforcing it.

"They were telling him he didn't have right to care, that he didn't have a right to protest. And I was enforcing it too; by thinking he should have known better, that he should have stopped. But why should Black people have to know better? Why should they have to know how to act? Why should they have to guard themselves against those who are sworn to protect citizens? No, Jeremy was doing what he had a right to do. The police were wrong, not him. When I stopped on their command, when I blamed Jeremy for his death, when I accept this country not treating all citizens as equals, I am enforcing second-class citizenry too. I am agreeing that Black people are second-class citizens, and Mother, there was nothing second-class about Jeremy. And if we would have had Black babies, there would have been nothing second-class about them either.

"I am going back to the dorm, Mother, back to school. Not tomorrow, but when my leg is able, I am going to school and back to work at 'The Blackman's Journal.' I was working on a story, an important story."

She digs the spoon into the custard and slides the loaded spoon into her mouth. Now that's sweet she thinks.

"Well," her mother pauses then says, "I'm going to tell you what my mother used to tell me . . . a hard head makes a soft sore ass."

Denise laughs, "And a sore shoulder and thigh."

Chapter Fourteen

Falcon City is eerily still with no pedestrians and sparse traffic. The late afternoon traffic is composed of mostly Falcon City police, news vans, and the military. People are not out walking the avenues or the streets.

"People are in shock," Melody says, commenting on the emptiness.

"Afraid. No one wants to be next. They witnessed the sheer power of the government. They thought they had a chance against the Falcon City police, a chance to win, a chance to make a change, but against a giant, a fat bully . . . they know their efforts are futile. The people of this city saw a neighborhood demolished. Who can fight against jets and bombs? They know they are outgunned."

He reaches for the radio, but decides against it. He would rather hear Melody's opinion.

"And you? Are you still feeling like a patriot?" She asks.

Maybe he should have cut the radio on. She went straight for the jugular. He looks out the window, stops at a blinking red light, raises his eyebrows and coughs all before he answers.

"Well? Don't play with me, Noble. You heard my question. Are you still feeling wrapped in the flag? Are you still Captain America?"

He drives by an army tank surrounded by Black and white soldiers.

"What I was part of has been destroyed, and it was destroyed by what I was loyal to. According to you, the country I love killed the man and the organization that pulled me from the mire of my own insanity. I have nothing to be loyal too."

His own words scare him. Is that really his reality? Is he a solider with no command? He turns off the avenue, avoiding looking at Melody.

"No, that's not true. You are a Black man, Noble. You have a people that need you desperately. You have many, a multitude, to be loyal to."

She sounds like Knight.

"You are going to like my friend."

Even in Knight's neighborhood, the streets are barren except for police. Breeze parks his car behind a white limo. In front of the limo, Breeze sees a police car and a black Mercedes. Knight's Lincoln Navigator is parked two houses down.

"My friend lost his son this morning. The police shot him down. He was good boy. He was the only person that I knew for their entire life. I was at the hospital when he was born. I saw him grow his first teeth and take his early steps, and now he is dead. Killed by police. I reacted by shooting six white students in the head this afternoon," he confesses to Melody.

"Before the campus shootings?"

"Yes."

"Why?"

He heavily exhales.

"Because I was hurting and I wanted balance. I wanted the other side to lose something. I told myself it wasn't racial, but it was. Those six white kids died because Jeremy died. I killed them all. Killing is what I do."

And the words ease his mind. The truth of the statement warms him like an old friend. Dr. Talbert is gone, but his old friend is still with him, and he smiles. Ok, he thinks, Melody may be right and wrong: right about them surviving and wrong about him changing from an assassin. He sees no need to change that. Killing is part of him.

"No, killing was what we did. What we were trained to do. We are more than assassins. Those boys I killed at the hotel were my last assignment. But honestly, I did want to kill Agnes. I saw her creep into the doorway. I saw her raise her weapons on us, and I could have killed her, but I didn't because I was finished with the APS.

"Shooting the boys at the hotel was it for me. I completed my assignments to maintain this life, but the account is balanced. I killed for this life, and I am keeping it."

He admires her determination although he thinks it's misguided. She, like he, will always be a killer.

"You wanted to kill old Agnes?"

"She didn't creep into the room like an old lady, and she was always so smug whenever I had to go over there like she was better than I was, and that was how she was standing in the doorway, like she was about to eliminate some rodent pests. So yeah, I wanted to kill her ass."

He leans over and kisses her lips again. He likes kissing her.

It isn't Knight who answers the door, but the young Black woman who works at the journal with him. Mildred, Breeze remembers.

"Greetings," she says without a smile. "The others are in the kitchen. Just walk straight back."

She closes the door behind them and follows them through the small house.

At the kitchen table, Breeze sees Renaldo Banks, Brother Jackson, and the mayor of Falcon City - Andrew Redding. His is the only white face at the table. The gathering shocks Breeze, but he keeps his face emotionless.

Standing in front of the stove and next to the refrigerator are two Black police officers. Breeze recognizes one from this morning, the sergeant who saved the two white officers' lives.

There are no chairs left at the table, so Breeze and Melody stand in front of the sink and listen.

"We had no choice but to accept the military action. Our police were powerless against the numbers."

The mayor appears to be begging a case.

"But you managed to keep the University safe."

Banks grunts, sliding his chair back from the table.

"I know how that looks, but I am here trying to save what's left of our city. If your people continue to riot, the city will be destroyed. The military presence makes that quite clear. I am here to thank you for getting the people off the streets, but they must remain off the streets until order is restored. Mr. Banks, we released you in good faith."

"And the people are off the streets," Banks answers.

"Yes, but we need a public announcement, one calling for continued peace."

"To be clear," Knight interrupts, "all charges are being dropped against Banks and his organization?"

"Yes, that has been done. The information provided by agent Jackson of the FBI exonerated them completely, and that same information will lead to the upcoming arrest of several of our own."

Breeze looks to Brother Jackson, an FBI agent. "Damn," he whispers.

"Yep," Melody answers also in a whisper.

"When do you want the statement?" Banks asks, pulling his red locks back from his Malcolm X-colored face.

"Now, we want you to make it from police headquarters . . . as a show of cooperation."

"And the school closing review board?" Knight interrupts again.

"Yes, headed by you and a team of your picking."

Banks looks to Knight who affirms with a nod.

"Ok, let's, go." Banks stands from his chair. "I will do what I can."

He leaves and is followed by the mayor and the police officers.

Brother Jackson looks to Breeze. "Noble," he greets.

"Jackson," Breeze answers, purposely dropping the 'Brother.'

"Dr. Talbert was killed." Brother Jackson announces, looking at Breeze, then at Melody.

Breeze searches his face for the slightest amusement. If he sees any, he is prepared to end Jackson's life for Dr. Talbert's, but Jackson's face is emotionally flat.

"And I'm guessing several others," Melody states.

"You're *guessing* correctly, Melody Richards."

He looks at her with recognition, but she doesn't look away.

"And the APS?" Melody continues.

Now Breeze sees Jackson smile, "APS . . . what, that think-tank from D.C.? The American Purist Society. Oh, I hear they have been dissolved - funding issues."

"And their employees?" she asks.

"Non-consequential. The FBI was only concerned with the principals and financing. Chop off the head and the body dies, but rumor has it that the FBI may be recruiting from the staff."

He glances from Breeze to Melody and back to Breeze.

"I'll be in touch when I hear more."

He stands from the table.

"Going downtown to help with the statement. You going, Knight?"

Knight stares at him hard for seconds, "No, Brother Jackson. I am in for the evening. That was enough police, politicians, and federal agents for one day. Matter of fact, I think I am at my limit for the year."

It sounded humorous, but Knight isn't laughing.

Jackson leaves and Breeze and Melody sit at the kitchen table.

"What was Jackson talking about, the APS?" Knight asks Breeze.

"Nothing, just a think-tank Dr. Talbert had me involved in."

"Yeah right, just a think-tank. The FBI is aware of its principals and finances, the Federal Bureau of

Investigation is considering recruiting from its former employees - and why would an FBI agent even know of Dr. Talbert's death? Why mention it to you in almost a threatening tone? Come on, Noble. I was born at night but not last night."

Knight looks from Breeze to Melody and back to Breeze for answers.

When none are offered, he wipes his hand across the crown of his baldhead and says, "Loose lips ain't sinking no ships up in here, huh? Ok, whatever, brother, there has been a shroud of mystery around you since undergrad, and I'm not certain I want it uncovered. I think I am safer in the dark." He moves his attention to Melody, "And please forgive the good doctor's rudeness. My name is Foster Knight." He extends his hand to shake.

"Oh," Melody smiles and extends her hand, "I am Melody Richards, Noble's girlfriend."

Breeze's faces opens up a grin, and so does Knight's.

"Really? Well that is good news. The brother is in need of some female guidance in his life. If any man needs a woman, it is Breeze. Did he tell you he brought his condo with the demo furniture? I think the only thing he added were sheets and towels, and all the man dresses in are suits. He needs you in life, Ms. Richards. God, he needs you."

Mildred comes into the kitchen.

"Mr. Knight, the plates of food I brought you over are in the refrigerator, and the mayor told me to tell you there will be a full investigation of Jeremy's shooting. I called the funeral home where my brother works, so they are going to contact you tomorrow. Are you sure you want to do all of this so soon?"

She makes the statements and asks the question from the doorway, not fully entering the kitchen.

"Yes, baby, the sooner the better," Knight answers, not looking at her or anyone else in the kitchen, but holding his head up towards the ceiling, obviously fighting back tears. "Jeremy is gone. No sense in dragging it all out, baby."

"Ok, sir. Well, I'm going to head on home. I will turn the bottom lock, but you be sure to lock up, Mr. Knight. These thugs around here ain't stop stealing."

"I will, baby."

She turns and leaves, and they hear the front door slam closed.

"How are you holding up, man?" Breeze directs the question to Knight.

"Shit brother, I can't tell you really. Everything has been moving so fast. I hate to say this, but you know the police shot our little white intern too, so that's why city will investigate. My son's death won't get swept under the rug because a white girl was shot with him."

"Yes, that's sad, but the good part is the mayor knows you now." Breeze confirms.

"Man, he knew me before. I was one of the first people he called to negotiate Banks' release. I didn't know he knew who I was, but he knew."

"I think you can credit that to Brother Jackson," Breeze says pensively.

"You mean Special Agent Jackson," Melody corrects.

"Yes, Mr. FBI. Who knew?" Breeze says looking her in the eye.

Knight raps on the table with his knuckles.

"I suspected something. He was too eager to get involved, and he always had money to assist, but no job. But . . . a roach fart would have knocked me over when he came through my front door with the mayor and Banks.

"So, Dr. Talbert got killed at the University?"

"Yes, we saw his house get bombed."

"Bombed?"

"You heard me. Wiped from the face of the earth."

"Damn, sorry to hear that, brother. I know he was important to you. How will his death affect your tenure?"

"It shouldn't," Melody answers for Breeze. "I filed all the necessary paperwork yesterday."

"You work at the University?"

"I am or I was Dr. Talbert's secretary."

"Damn, Breeze, you crossing your *T*s and dotting your *I*s, ain't cha, boy?"

Breeze answers, smiling, "No, man, it just worked out that way." Noticing his own smile.

Melody, being in her company, being associated with her, has him smiling more than he has in years. He would be angry, murderously so, if she were not with him. Dr. Talbert brought him from nothing to life; someone, no, a number of people, should have died to balance Breeze's loss.

"Is there anything you need tonight, man?" Breeze asks Knight.

"Naw Breeze, I am just going to spend some time talking to my God, praying for some acceptance and peace." He looks to the ceiling, to the window over the sink, to Melody, then back to Breeze.

"You know, I came home from that hospital and loaded up my shotgun and my .38. But the good lord sent Mildred over here, and she talked me down, and then the mayor called and I got all wrapped up into that situation.

"Man, white people sure are polite when they need something from you. Mayor Redding talked to me like I was the Governor. You know, we have been trying for over a year to get a school closing adversary board, but after people picked up guns and went to shooting police and white racists, the mayor's whole attitude changed. It was like them bombs and bullets shook some reason loose in his head."

"Something got shook loose, that's for sure," Melody says.

Breeze smiles at her statement. She is never hesitant to speak her mind. Watching her lips, and the muscles in her bright face move, he has the desire to kiss her, really kiss her, and to be soothed by her touch.

"Ok, man, we're going to head on out too," Breeze announces.

"Oh ok, so you know you are going to be on the school closing board, right?"

It was a question and a declaration.

"No problem, man. I will be honored."

Dr. Talbert's order to cease and desist in regard to the school closing protest has been nullified by his death and the APS's destruction. His mind goes to Melody's words: "You have a people who need you desperately."

While driving her home, Breeze finds it hard to keep his eyes on the road. When Melody speaks, he wants to be looking at her. He likes how her face moves, especially her lips.

"Do you think anything will really change?" she asks.

"Things have already changed."

He is thinking about his life: no APS, no Dr. Talbert, and now Melody and Knight. He enjoys community work, but to do it without the APS agenda in mind will be different. To work to help the community, really help will be different.

"No, I mean for the community. Do you think things will get better?"

"Yes, I do. Banks is out of jail. Afro-Americans in Falcon City will see that as a win, and the mayor said something about people going to jail. The community will respond to that too. Small wins motivate movement. Things were happening with Banks already. So with his return, the community should be active."

Banks not being dead, as the APS wanted, will bring change; he is certain of that.

"And what about Special Agent Jackson?" She asks.

"What about him?"

"Do you think he is a threat to us?"

"No, I think he is going to offer us jobs."

"Would you work for the FBI?"

"In a heartbeat."

"Not me, no way, enough is enough. Let's get burgers," Melody says pointing to a hamburger restaurant's drive thru.

Breeze turns into the restaurant, but the place is closed.

"Dang, I have never seen them closed before," Melody sighs. "I'm hungry."

"I could eat, too, but the workers are probably scared to come to work."

"Or they were in the riot, fighting for their lives."

"Fighting for the lives? Really?"

"Yeah, their lives, their rights. People are tired of this shit: police shooting people, low-ass wages or no damn jobs, and horrible-ass schools. It's time to riot."

When he looks at her, he sees the muscles in her face tightening. She is really upset he thinks, and he likes that.

"Kind of committed, huh?"

"I don't know what I am, Noble. But I know what I am not."

"An assassin?"

"Right."

"I have some food at my place."

"Are you inviting me over?"

"Yes, I am."

"What do you have?"

"Beans, turkey legs, salad stuff, apples, corn, and some rice."

"Sounds more healthy than tasty. Can you cook?"

"Sort of, at least good enough to eat. Hey, ummm, it's getting dark, and ummm, I really don't want to travel at night with all the unrest. You don't mind spending the night, do you?"

He quickly looks at her, then out the window, then back at her.

"Nope, not as long as you feed me," she answers.

Again she makes him smile. She will be the first female guest and only his second guest.

When they get to his area of the Falcon City, Melody says, "A person wouldn't even know there were riots in the city looking around here. People are out strolling and walking their damn dogs like nothing is wrong."

"Nothing is wrong for them. People over here are not fighting for their lives."

"Must be nice."

Soothed doesn't quiet describe the peace that has blanketed Breeze. His bed never felt as comfortable, his skin never felt so alive, and his nose has never provided him with such a pleasant, gentle fragrance as that of Melody. Her head is between his shoulder and bicep, and he is breathing her in. She smells like peaches and coconuts.

"It has been awhile, huh?" she asks.

"Why do you say that?"

"Because, Noble, we did it three times back to back, and at the hospital you would only do it once."

"I had medicine in my system then. We were lucky to do it at all, but yes, it has been awhile," he admits.

"For me too. It's just so hard to get close enough to be intimate, but I know you. You know?"

"Yes, we have a history."

"We do, and honestly, I do like your new shiny suit."

She laughs and moves off of his shoulder and out of the bed. She stands and stretches her arms toward the ceiling. He looks at her firm, athletic body. Every three months an APS agent has to take a physical stamina test. Her body tone tells him she passed, probably scored better than he.

"I like your body, your face, your lips, and how you make me feel," he was thinking those things, but he wasn't planning on saying them; they just came out of his mouth.

He sits up in the bed a little startled. He usually has better control over thoughts that become verbal.

"And how is that? How do I make you feel?"

She puts her leg on the bed and bends her head to her knee.

Breeze wants to be accurate in his answer, and he wants to say what he has evaluated, not his first thoughts, so he takes a couple of seconds to think before he speaks.

She stops stretching and looks at him, waiting.

"You make me feel part of, you make me feel attached, you make me feel like I was missing something but found it. You make how I see the world better. You make me think that I can exist without Dr. Talbert and the APS. You make me proud of myself."

He sees her smile.

"You should be proud of yourself, Noble. You are a Black with a Ph.D. in racist-ass America. You are published, your students respect you, staff is envious of your accomplishments, and you are a community activist. You, Dr. Noble Breeze, are the man."

Her words make him grin.

"So," he hesitates to consider the question.

She waits.

"You know you are killing me with these pregnant pauses, right?"

He exhales.

"I just want to say it right. So, since we obviously have a thing going on here, and since we do have a history, and since you have informed my best friend that you are my girlfriend, and since I desperately desire you near me . . . what do you think about moving in?"

He had to ask her because the question was eating itself out of his mind. She soothes him in a way nothing or no one else does. She brings confusion to his mind, but she settles his thinking as well. He didn't know he needed her until he had her.

"Here, in this lily-white neighborhood? You want me to move in here with you?"

"Yes, I do."

"How much is the rent?"

"I have a mortgage, $2600 a month."

"Oh, I only pay $850 for rent. Stepping up to $1300 would be a bit difficult."

"No, I am paying the mortgage now without you. I am not asking you to be my roommate. I am asking you to be my woman."

He likes how the statement sounds outside of his mind, his woman.

"Your woman?" She crosses her arms across her half-a-watermelon-sized breast. "Well, if I become your woman and move in here with you, I have some requirements . . ."

She gives him a pregnant pause.

He sits waiting, and waiting, and waiting.

"What?" he blurts out, "What requirements?"

She laughs and takes her leg from the bed and drops her arms from her breast.

"Ok, here goes."

She opens her palm and starts counting down on her fingers.

"First, you have to be finished killing. Second, you cannot go to work for the FBI. Third, you must be satisfied with being a university professor only, with no clandestine activities at all, and finally, you must continue your Black community activities. If you can meet all these stipulations, you will have some live-in pussy."

When she said live-in pussy, his dick responded by thickening again. Less than two hours ago, he was considering killing her. He is extremely grateful that he didn't.

"What, no church service?"

She laughs again.

"Later. That will come later for both of us."

She sits back down on the bed.

"We are cut from the same cloth, Noble. We both know that. We have overcome similar sicknesses. Together, I think we can make it, but we have to be on the same page. I am through killing, and you must be too."

He thinks about the guns under the bed. He thinks about working for the FBI. He thinks about his love for America, about being a patriot, and asks, "but what if our country needs us?"

She leans over and puts her head on his shoulder.

"Mmph, still wrapped in that flag, huh? You can answer the call of your country without being an assassin or an agent for the FBI. Black people are Americans, Noble. By helping the community, you are helping the country."

She has a point, he thinks, looking down into her face, and he doesn't want to lose the feeling that comes from them being together.

"Will you kill in self-defense?" he asks her.

"If I have too. What I am finished with Noble, is being an assassin, and I don't want a man who is an assassin, but I do expect you to protect yourself and me. I am not a pacifist, but neither am I a killer for hire."

"So when would you move in?"

"Is that a yes to no more killing and no FBI?"

He is not going to turn down the FBI if they make him an offer, but he does want Melody to live with him, so he lies with a smile and says, "Yes . . . to all your demands."

Chapter Fifteen

What she wants from a new day isn't there. Jeremy is dead. The shower wasn't refreshing, the cantaloupe wasn't sweet, and the cab driver is refusing to take a credit card or break her hundred-dollar bill. Instead of going in and out of the apartment as she planned, they have to go to a gas station to break the hundred-dollar bill. The cabby wants to be paid for bringing her to the apartment even though he agreed to wait for her to come out.

The neighborhood is smoldering in the early morning. She'd gotten out of the bed before her parents awoke. She didn't sleep a wink. Her mind raced with thoughts of her story. All her notes were on her laptop in the apartment, and she wanted her phone.

She brings a bag of chips and a pop to the gas station counter. The skinny attendant frowns at the hundred-dollar bill.

"The bank is closed. We couldn't get any change. Do you have anything smaller?"

"Nope."

"Do you want anything else?"

"Nope."

He gives her a fifty, two twenties, and six dollars in quarters. She limps from the gas station store to the cab. She noticed the cabby cut the meter off when she got to the apartment and didn't run it from the apartment to the gas station. She likes that.

She is expecting to see yellow tape and chalk outlines. She sees neither. She pays the cabby and tells him, "Wait."

"Yeah, I told you I would."

He is a young black man, Denise guesses he is around twenty-five. She wonders whether he was involved in the riots.

When she looks to the street in front of the building, she sees the dark spot that was Clinton. His car is still there, burned to a wreck. On the curb, she sees Jeremy's blood. She limps up the walkway.

Her laptop is still on the futon. Bending down to it and her phone is painful, but she gets both. She fights against the impulse to stay and cry. She will let Mr. Knight bring her the other things. She pulls the door close and locks it.

She tells the cabby, "6414 Spring Grove Avenue."

"You got it; that's The Blackman's Journal, ain't it? I read that paper every week. They write about the truth. You work there?"

"Yep, I'm a reporter."

"Wow, you gonna write about the riots?"

"Without a doubt."

"Well, I know y'all gonna tell the truth about everything. I didn't know white people worked there, but I guess it doesn't make a difference what color the writer is as long as they tell the truth. Y'all did a good job on the school closings. People needed to know about the mess the city was and is doing. My son goes to a school in High-bolt; the one Banks and the Freedom Protestors kept open. I rallied with them because of y'all's article. Y'all gave me information that I didn't know. I didn't know people could fight against schools closing. I always thought the city did what it wanted and that was that, but now, I know better because The Blackman's Journal got me in touch with Banks and his people. You got an important job."

"I know, and thank you. My boyfriend wrote those articles, he and his father."

"Well, you tell them to keep up the good work, and tell them that I'm going to keep reading the paper, and I got my wife and my folks reading now. Yeah, I like that paper. Y'all tell the truth."

Denise walks into the Journal office and sees Mildred and Mr. Knight sitting behind desks eating breakfast sandwiches.

"What, no classes?" Mildred asks.

"Don't know, didn't check."

She walks to her desk, trying her best not to limp. She doesn't want Mr. Knight to send her home. She sits without a groan or moan, places her laptop on the desk and opens it.

"What are you wearing?" Mildred asks.

"One of my mother's gym outfits. She likes pink."

"Girl, you need to get that back to her ASAP."

"What are you doing here, Denise?" Knight asks, biting into a sandwich.

"The same as you, Mr. Knight. I have a story to write."

"The murdered police story?"

He sits back in the chair.

"In part, but I was thinking more of a cause and effect piece."

She sees his eyebrows go up.

"Explain."

"Instead of investigating *who*, I am thinking about the *why* angle. The *why* is the bigger problem. The *who* stems from the *why*. Yesterday's riots gave us *who*'s. More than one person attacked the police, but I want to show that the same *why* sparked their actions. Identifying the *why* brings knowledge. I want to write about *why* the people rioted. I think that is more needed."

"Mmph, people already know why," he says.

"Some people, not all people, and it always helps to have feelings made valid, and identifying the *why* in print assists with that validity. Yes, people know injustice exists, but pointing to specific problems, I believe, will bring cohesion between like-minded people. When people read what has been bothering them in print, when their problem is shared through exposure, a rallying call is sounded."

A big smile appears across Knight's face.

"Mmph, so you are wanting to be a bugler, a real journalist, huh?" Knight takes another bite from his sandwich.

"I like that metaphor, bugler."

"Yeah, when I started that was my attitude, and that was what I tried passed on to my son. You are onto something, Denise. Outline the story for me, and we will go from there."

She cuts on her laptop and scoots her chair closer to the desk.

"And your father called."

"Did he?"

"He said we should be expecting you and asked if I could drive you home."

"What did you tell him, sir?"

"I told him no problem, and it would be good to have you at work."

Mildred tosses a breakfast sandwich on her desk.

"Mr. Knight ordered you one, too."

Chapter Sixteen

Breeze has an eight o'clock class, and Melody is due to work at seven-thirty. They are standing at the doors of the Camry when a black SUV pulls up beside Breeze in the street. The passenger window rolls and they see Brother Jackson.

"Give her the keys, Breeze. She can drive herself to work. We need to meet."

Melody walks into the street and directly to the passenger window.

"He has an eight o'clock class. I am sure your meeting can wait."

"Cutie, City University classes have been cancelled for the week, but administrative staff has been called in, and guess what, you have been assigned to Dr. Noble Breeze. You should get the news around ten-thirty. Act surprised."

He looks from her to Breeze.

"Get in, Noble."

The back door of the SUV swings open.

Breeze hands Melody the keys.

"The parking key pass is above the visor."

He avoids eye contact with her and gets into the SUV.

"So, she's moving in with you. There is nothing better than live-in pussy. But what the fuck does she have against the Bureau? Shit, after being with those

APS crazies you would think she would jump at the chance to do some real work."

Breeze had never swept his apartment for listening devices. There was no need. The APS did the surveying. He never considered them being surveyed or investigated.

"That was the most chatter you had in your place in over a year, besides that fanatical Knight and all his Black people community bullshit. Look, Breeze, we know who you are and who you were. We know what you did to get the attention of the APS, we know what you did for the APS, but more importantly, we know what you are capable of doing."

There is a Black agent sitting next to Breeze, two white agents behind him, and a Mexican agent driving Special Agent Jackson.

"We are not interested in disturbing the life the APS created for you. We want that life to continue. We have arranged a three-month sabbatical for your training. When you return, Melody Richards will be your full-time secretary. Your tenure has been secured. You will be notified this afternoon along with your sabbatical approval. What we are offering you is what you thought you had with the APS. You won't be a contract killer with us. You will be an FBI agent."

"I am forty-one years old."

"We know how old you are, Breeze."

"Where will I be for the three months?"

"Ouantico, Virginia, then DC, and finally New York."

"When would I leave?"

"This afternoon."

"Melody will leave me."

"Man, you just got her. She ain't going nowhere. She will adapt, trust me."

Without looking back at Breeze, Jackson hands him an envelope over his shoulder. "Your plane ticket. Don't pack. When you land, you will be met at the airport."

"How did you know I would I agree?"

"You are a patriot, Breeze, through and through."

Breeze is sitting at the desk in his office looking at the airplane ticket, business class. He hasn't called Melody. What if he had said no? They probably would have killed him, but who knows. Why didn't they make the offer to Melody, too? Because they heard her talking last night, his car must be bugged too. He is excited about the opportunity. There is no denying it.

With the APS gone, the FBI is a graduation of sorts, the next level of his patriotism. Jackson said it: he is a patriot through and through. The FBI wants him, even though they know about all of him. He is part of the status quo, and he will protect it.

America has embraced him again, accepting him and wanting his skills. It's not about color; it's about

169

loyalty. In the SUV were Black, white and Mexican agents, all patriots. Dr. Talbert had trained him well, making him a patriot the FBI would want.

His office door opens and Melody enters.

"Your tenure was unanimously approved - not one objection - amazing. And this three-month sabbatical approval came through as well, amazing again. When do you leave? And is it the FBI?"

"Soon, in a couple of hours."

"And?"

"Yes, it is the FBI."

"Are you forcing yourself to hold back a happy smile?"

He laughs.

"Yes, no, well, yes, sort of. I want to be happy, but I don't want you upset."

"Noble, all we did was fuck."

She exhales, and sits in the chair in front of the desk.

"No, we made plans."

She slides his car keys across the desk.

"Not really."

He looks down at the keys.

"No, you keep those; the condo keys are on there as well. I want you to keep the car while I'm gone, and I need a ride to the airport, and you are going to need to sweep the place and the car for bugs."

He's talking as if he doesn't know she is refusing to move in.

"I'm not moving in, especially with you leaving for a three-month camp-out sponsored by the FBI."

She's funny he thinks.

"A camp-out, huh? I think they refer to it as training." He grins, "Why wouldn't you move in? My place is better than your place, and it's rent-free for three months. You can save a substantial amount of money."

"Wait . . . what do you mean, sweep the place for bugs?"

"Yes, you would have to. They heard everything we said last night, so that means the car and my condo are bugged, and probably your place too. They have been investigating the APS for . . . I don't know how long."

"Wow, and you still going to work for them?"

"Why wouldn't I?"

"Because they have no respect for anyone's civil rights. And they probably killed your mentor. Wait, they heard us making love?"

"They don't care about us individually; they were after the APS as an organization."

"How much do they know about us?"

"Everything."

"Everything?"

"Everything. They are the FBI."

"The truth is they probably have known about us all the time. I told you."

And she did. Her guess was a hundred percent right; he has no doubt the FBI assassinated Dr. Talbert and the other APS leaders.

"I think that would be an accurate assumption. Are you going to move in?"

He slides the keys back across the desk. And he pulls his holster and .9mm from the small of his back and slides them to her as well.

"I can't go to the airport with it."

Looking down at both the pistol and the keys she says, "It's funny because I am to sign a new lease this week. This is a good time to move."

"You will save a lot of money."

"Is that the only reason I should move in, Noble? To save some money?"

He doesn't answer with words. He looks at her intently hoping she can see the need in his eyes.

"I have told you only one lie, but now that lie is out in the open."

She sucks her teeth.

"I knew you were lying when you said you it. I know you."

He wants to smile, but he doesn't. He keeps his eyes on hers.

"Yes, I guess I want both things that make me happy, you and working for the FBI."

She sucks her teeth again.

"And you don't know if either one will make you happy: the FBI or me."

"You are right. Both will be learning experiences that I am sure will require some acceptance. But acceptance allows growth. We don't get everything we want from other people, life, or relationships. Our thing won't be perfect, but we will have a thing as opposed to not having one. Us being together is better for both of us. You know that and I know that. You said it yourself – we are cut from the same cloth. If I need you as much as I do, you must need me some.

"I will try my best to never lie to you again. I am going to work for the FBI, and I want you in my life, and I think you should move in because you like my shiny suit."

He sees her smile. He watches her pick up the keys and the pistol. She stands.

"I'll drive you to the airport."

He watches the sway of her hips as he exits his office.

There is nothing he needs to go back to condo for. He will tell Melody about the gun safe under the bed. It will be good to have her to come home to. Three months of FBI training, he could live through that.

He stands from his desk and decides to take a brief walk around campus to kill some time. Someone knocks on his office door but doesn't wait for him to answer or open it. In walks the department co-chair, Dr. Saltine.

He clears his throat at the door, and pushes his blonde hair back from his eyes while walking to Breeze. Standing in front of Breeze's desk, he says, "I don't who you are or who you know, or what kind of affirmative action bullshit this is, but I was next in line for a full-time secretary. As department co-chair, I shouldn't be sharing a secretary with four other professors. I am expecting you to refuse the secretary's appointment, so she will come to me. Obviously something has gone wrong in the system. I need your signature on this form denying the appointment. I was clearly next in line."

He's standing before Breeze with red ears and neck and his upper body torso is trembling slightly. Being passed over for the secretary has obviously upset him.

Breeze doesn't need a secretary. The departmental, team player thing to do would be to sign the paper, but as an FBI recruit, a former decorated APS agent, a published professor, the boyfriend of an extremely attractive woman, and as a Black Ph.D. in racist America, Breeze asks, "Why should I?"

The professor huffs, repeatedly blinks his eyes and says, "Because I was next. Something has gone wrong with Talbert's unexpected death and things are all mixed up, but as the co-chair, the secretary should be mine."

But, you are not being recruited by the FBI Breeze thinks. He smiles inwardly. There is privilege with being a patriot, a true American. He decides to keep Melody as his secretary because he deserves her.

"Mm, this is what I am willing to do. I'm leaving this afternoon for a three-month sabbatical. For those ninety days, she can be your secretary, but when I return she will report to me."

"Sabbatical? I haven't been notified of any sabbatical for you. You just got tenure. All of this is highly irregular, and I am not going to stand for it. You are taking advantage of a situation," he says pointing his finger at Breeze. "You see, this is why I didn't want to sign off on to your tenure. You people get in and the rules change, and your race is so opportunistic. You are taking advantage of the riots and Talbert's death. Since our department is unsettled, you are taking advantage. I knew having a Black on staff would lead to problems. I was certain of it. Sign this paper like I am telling you so I can leave."

He slams the paper down on Breeze's desk.

"Like you are telling me?"

"Yes," he shouts, "Like I am telling you. I am the co-chair, soon to be chair. The secretary is mine."

His whole face is red.

Breeze's smile comes outward. This is what men like Dr. Saltine are fighting against, this power right here, this shift in the application of power. Due to the FBI involvement, Breeze is being granted more privilege, more access to power than Dr. Saltine. And this change is what people like Dr. Saltine are fighting against.

"Change is inevitable, Dr. Saltine."

"What? What on God's earth are you taking about? Sign the damn paper."

"No. I have told you what I am willing to do. Accept it or not."

He picks the paper up from the desk and hands it back to Dr. Saltine.

"Uppity," he says snatching the papers from Breeze's hand, "There was a time when you wouldn't have dared to sass me."

"Sass you? Man, get the hell out of my office before I bring you to a reality that will cripple your small mind, believe me."

Breeze doesn't feel the weight of the .9mm in the small of his back, and he is grateful.

Dr. Saltine is standing holding the paper in his hand, trembling.

"Are you refusing to sign this paper?"

"Yes, and to spare your life."

"My life?"

Breeze doesn't answer. He looks through Dr. Saltine's gray eyes. And by reflex, his hand goes to the small of his back. He envisions Dr. Saltine's head snapping back from the impact of a .9mm bullet.

Breeze guesses that Dr. Saltine senses something because he walks backward from his stare, not taking his eyes off of Breeze. He even tries to open the door still facing Breeze. He is fumbling backwards with the door handle. On a whim Breeze says, "Boo!"

Dr. Saltine rapidly turns and yanks the door open and flees the office.

Breeze knows he went too far, but it felt good. Good to be on the side of privilege, good to have power, and good to be considered valuable. Good to be an American, a true American.

He takes his hand from the small of his back.

"I will learn from the training. Threatening that man wasn't right."

His phone vibrates in his suit. He answers.

"Your flight is in two hours, Dr. Breeze. You should be on your way out now. And I told you the girl wasn't going anywhere," Jackson says.

"I'm leaving now."

Breeze hangs up, and walks from his office to Dr. Talbert's old office and Melody.

She is sitting in the outer office, smiling.

"What did you do to Dr. Saltine?"

"Nothing, just told him he couldn't have my woman."

Breeze grins standing in the doorway.

"Well, he certainly was flustered. He said something about me calling security, but when I told him I was taking you to the airport right now, he stormed out, saying he would call them himself."

"Are you ready?"

He stands watching his woman log off the computer.

"You know, three months is a long time when you are going to miss someone," he says.

"Ninety days, Dr. Breeze. I did a search for the Bureau's training. It's over in ninety days."

"So, you are going to miss me too?"

Walking from behind the desk she says, "I might, I just might," and walks into a kiss.

Made in the USA
Columbia, SC
24 May 2021